T0157366

Royally Courted

The Jury Summons

C.S. NOLAN

iUniverse LLC
Bloomington

Royally Courted
The Jury Summons

iUniverse books may be ordered through booksellers or by contacting:

iUniverse
1663 Liberty Drive
Bloomington, IN 47403
www.iuniverse.com
1-800-Authors (1-800-288-4677)

ISBN: 978-1-4759-3429-8 (sc)
ISBN: 978-1-4759-3430-4 (e)
ISBN: 978-1-4759-3431-1 (dj)

Printed in the United States of America

iUniverse rev. date: 7/8/2012

Contents

Chapter 1: Althea

*A*lthea walked solemnly to the edge of the steep Irish Moher cliffs, her head bowed ever so slightly, eyes peering to the sea, every day looking, always looking. The cool ocean breezes moved her hair about, but her head was still and strong. This walk was a part of her daily routine. She knew in her heart that regardless of the absence of her beloved, their souls would always be united. Slowly, she walked the rugged path, strewn with rocks and bits of shrubbery, taking each step with care and heartfelt direction. As she neared the steep edge, of the basalt-lined, weather-beaten cliffs, Althea raised her handsome head, her dark eyes scanning the blue Atlantic... gazing into the vast horizon looking for the ship that would bring forth her world.

The rhythmic waves thundered a bold greeting. Althea could feel the massive vibration through her strong limbs, and the sound rekindled memories of the *Scottish Queen* and her voyage to this treasured Irish Island. This sound would forever echo in her mind and heart. As she looked and waited, a lone teardrop, like the dew on a rose, rolled down her olive wind-nipped cheek. She never shuddered or made a sound, but her pounding heart yearned for the vision of the distant ship approaching the harbor.

Thinking about the harbor Althea recalled, "Many a ship had been taken here, and a memorial chapel had been built in honor of the victims of a tragic shipwreck...

She had doubts of his return, with war still raging throughout Europe and the coastal dangers, but her hope remained forever intact.

She strained her eyes until her tear-stained face dried, leaving gentle tracks of her unending love. The Irish wind was at her back, and the ebb and flow of the waves seemed comforting, as if they were saying, "Until tomorrow, dear heart. We wait for you and wish you well."

Althea's mind answered with heartfelt longing, "Oh, Grand Ocean, take care of my love and let him return to me." As Althea's thoughts turned to returning to the castle and her treasured daughters, she knew her soul and Matthew's were forever united, and their love would journey wherever their hearts and souls wandered. She felt the hope of a new day.

As she returned to the path, she reflected on the happiness she withheld, Rose and Sophie—the children that bonded she and Matthew's eternal love.

Through the eyes of these girls, their love would always exist. Her heart was filled with both sadness and joy, a mixture of emotions so true to the human spirit. Their children would forever preserve the sacred love that would be uncovered throughout time.

Her brisk walk ended at a small well, dug deep into the rich Irish soil. Here, fresh, ice-cold water flowed freely. Althea slowly pulled the rope on an old wooden bucket to retrieve the spring water from the deep well. This was the same spring that fed the beautiful waterfall on the hidden path to the castle. She rejoiced in the refreshment, as had many a thirsty soul.

She approached the old fortress fondly, all surrounded by green grasses and moss growing gracefully between the old stones. She moved naturally, and climbed the rugged stone steps, long lived and strong, only faintly showing signs of wear after hundreds of years.

She entered the stone kitchen and placed a brick of peat moss on the fireplace grate, igniting the fire to a hot blaze. It eventually would burn down to glowing embers, keeping all that dwelled there warm and safe. Althea sat wearily on a heavy wooden chair, one that was placed by the great hearth for those who needed a moment to warm their bodies and revive a dampened soul.

The bright afternoon had turned to dusk, and the sky began to darken. She watched the fire slowly begin to blaze and crackle. Despite the hard wooden seat, she felt warm and comfortable, knowing that many a family member had sat here. Somehow, she felt as if Matthew was embracing her, and their love filled her heart with love.

Leaning to the side, she rested her head against the warm stones of the hearth. She thought fondly of her love. With all her might she wished she and Mathew were reunited, here and now. As she gazed into the blazing fire, her thoughts began to wander. She closed her eyes and began to dream of days long past.

***

Althea was young and eager to embrace the adventures of life. Although her family was not wealthy, they had enough to live comfortably.

Residing along the southern French coastal ridge, Cote de Azur, life was pleasant. The traffic of foreign travelers brought trade and commerce to the small fishing village. Shops were always busy, and the fishermen always had enough fish to meet the needs of the demanding merchants. A robust economy existed, not just from the trade, but also from the locals who worked and traveled throughout the coastal regions. They were farmers, fishermen, bakers, parents, children, artists, writers and navigators, all dreaming of achievement and happiness. Althea's father, Jon Paul, was a business owner and was a very well-known and trusted citizen in the area. He had acquired a small tavern that served food and beverages. This small tavern served many hungry sailors, merchants, and anyone who entered this well-known place of congregation.

Jon Paul was a robust and sincere man who had married well above his family's expectations. He loved and was greatly devoted to Althea's mother, Ginevra. She came from a noble family that had suffered financially through the changing times. Their marriage was celebrated by all, because a love so fine and strong created a strong French society. Their offspring would enrich their lives. Althea had two older brothers both strong and intelligent. They attended a school of law and government in Paris. Their lives, as well as the lives of Althea and her parents were filled with service and gratitude. In this charming French fishing village the people thrived and here they were able to have families, study art, and serve their fellow man or not. They owned their good life, and it was sweet.

This community thrived gracefully until the Reformation Movement. In the early 1600s, political strife began to create friction, throughout Europe. Even the small villages suffered. Sailors from afar brought news of the devastating war—a type of religious reformation, Europe was suffering from this profound political event that created turbulence between the Catholics and the Protestants. This religious struggle had all torn apart between the church and the new laws demanded by their young king. King Raymond was not pleased with the laws of marriage and divorce. He had asked the church to make changes so he could marry his new mistress. The church would not appease him and did not make the changes he so demanded. With that in mind, the country became hostile and rebellious because King Raymond began to challenge the power of the church demanding changes in office, new powers terminating old powers and sometimes with the loss of a head.

The counterattack from the opposing forces, the church and their followers became rebellious in the form of looting, burning, and killing. Many villages and people tried to remain neutral, not wanting to suffer at the hands of a vicious rebellion.

Cote de Azur was only but one of the many villages trying to remain free from political standing. They did their best to live and let live, however, opposing forces wanted to create strife and trouble and all would suffer in this time of religious change.

Althea's parents became concerned about their village and their family's welfare. Jon Paul and Ginevra masked their fear, allowing their children to not see their worry and concern for the future.

Both boys were in the protection of their prestigious school, and Althea was kept busy with her studies, the upkeep of the residence, and the care of her delicate mother. The constant state of worry for her children's safety and the reminders of her earlier tormented life began to create a sickness in Ginevra. The noble life of a Royal Parisian was not as splendid as all had thought. Her marriage to Althea's father had been her sanctuary, but these troubled times manifested a type of illness that left her without the ability to care for the home or the family, so Althea's responsibility was great and her cooperation essential. Much to their mother's fears, her children were very aware of the circumstances.

The days in the village continued as before but now with guarded apprehension. Jon Paul had been secretly commissioned to lead a small defense of civilians to guard the vulnerable village. Many local citizens were against forming an alliance to oppose the government. So, his weekly meetings were done in utmost privacy, and the villagers remained silent, but as fear began to brew, the news leaked of their special forces, and chaos began to seat itself within the villagers. Distrust infiltrated the once serene village, and the daily routine became more difficult to maintain.

Ginevra had been secretly blackmailed to demand that her husband forbid his participation in this alliance. Her blackmailers were set on Gindevra's success. Little to her knowledge, she had been poisoned when she was unable to prohibit Jon Paul's retreat. He had been successful and had established a fighting force to oppose the powers of the state and government. Ginerva had been persecuted by her blackmailers, and time was not on her side.

Jon Paul's contribution to a strong and steadfast group of men ready to fight and defend their village became well known and was feared by those that wanted a neutral force. As Ginevra became sicker, Jon Paul was extremely concerned about her. Each day, her condition became worse, and she began to fade in and out of reality. She had lost weight, and her eyes began to look sunken. Her face was ashen, as if death were leading her slowly to a path of never-ending shadows. Little did he know, his own actions contributed to her debilitating illness.

Althea was concerned and devastated about her mother's declining health, and she did everything possible to help her become well again. Althea tried to contact many doctors, they came to her aid, but never did Ginevra regain the vigorous health she had once maintained. The illness was a mystery, a mystery contrived and deceitful.

Althea, like her mother had once been, had a strong spirit. She did everything in her power to help her, but to no avail. Althea was also lively and outgoing like Jon Paul, and she also suffered trying to help her mother of this horrible omen. The secret poisoning came from a mysterious group and never did she have any awareness of such scandal.

Althea spent most of her time with her mother, attending her diligently, and yet found time to attend the local school. She also spent evenings helping her father in the tavern. Her routine was hurried, and she had very little time for herself. As a young lady, she wanted to be with her peers, but her devotion to her family took priority. Althea was aware of and began to understand the possibilities of a battle in her coastal village. Even with this overwhelming gloom, she carried inside her a special spark of optimism and enthusiasm. She enjoyed her schooling and spent many late nights writing. She was especially talented with poetry and short stories. Her poetry had captured her teacher's attention and was beginning to gain notoriety.

She was also a student of language and could speak fluently in several languages other than her eloquent French. Her mother was adamant about Althea's education, both as a scholar and a lady. The noble blood would flourish in this young woman.

She knew the patrons and they considered her to be a mixture of beauty, brains, and courage. She would indeed be a fine lady, full of grace and insight.

Jon Paul realized that Althea was at the age where she could leave home, marry, and begin a family of her own. He also regretted the fact that Althea did not seem to feel the need to court any suitors that came her way, she was dedicated to her family and wanted to stay close to assist with their likelihood. And indeed there were fine young men interested and willing, but again, Althea was not receptive to their advances.

After a time, most let her be, and she seemed quite content with that—until her feelings began to develop around a young sea captain, Matthew MacDonnell of Scotland. He became the light of her life, as he was to many persons of the village. His knowledge and experience of navigating the seas interested the villagers and the sailors.

Matthew was confident and his voice calm and clear. He had a genuine smile and was friendly and congenial to others, regardless of their age or their walk of life, be it rich or poor. He was gentle with the curious children, delighting them with trinkets that he had collected along his voyages from afar. To the elderly and the sad, he listened, and rarely gave advice, but humbly acknowledged their apprehension or their eccentricities. Althea admired his worldliness and his humble and confident personality. His generosity and thoughtfulness warmed her heart, but most of all she was overjoyed to see his rapport with her father.

Despite his gallantry, Althea did recognize his flaw, he was a lonely man with a deep burden. His golden heart had a frozen aura. She would observe him, when he was not aware and had noticed he would look out and his mind would wander, the lines on his forehead told her he was not at peace and that he was troubled by something or someone. He had never shared this with her verbally, but Althea knew, and so did Jon Paul...

Althea and Matthew had a special friendship; they could talk of nothing and yet feel a great sense of satisfaction. Althea would ask Matthew gently, "What bothers you, my friend?" Matthew would look into Althea's dark brown eyes and reply, "My beautiful Althea, what could ever be my trouble with your grace around me?" Althea would smile warmly, but she knew Matthew was unsettled. She did not pry but accepted his quiet turmoil.

With an ailing wife and both sons away from home, Jon Paul was greatly burdened, and Matthew's friendship with Althea reassured him that Althea would always have an advocate. Jon Paul had asked Matthew to watch over Althea—he wanted to be certain that if the village should become involved in a battle and he were to perish, Althea and Genevra would be cared for. When Althea heard of her father's request, she laughed at the thought of needing an advocate. She was an independent lady and could take care of herself—she did not need aid. Inwardly, however, she was relieved that her father had spoken to Matthew, and indeed, Matthew was most willing to take this responsibility. He was quite fond of Althea, like a sister, but as Althea began to blossom, Matthew became more drawn to her as a kindred sprite and perhaps the lady of his dreams.

He loved her fierce independence and her gentle spirit. Her writing was impressive, and he began to spend more time with her. His visits to the village became more frequent, and his stays were always planned to be close to Althea and her family. He and Althea would spend endless time walking on the beach, hand in hand, sometimes talking, sometimes not. They found ways to be together, but Matthew began to feel an old thorn in his side... the sore of the thorn that never heals, Matthew was hindered by the thought that his family had betrothed him in marriage when he was a young lad. He had adamantly disagreed with them and had become quite rebellious. He had told his parents that he would not fulfill the betrothal. This was one of the reasons he had decided to travel, and begin a life in the military. His father wanted him near home, as did his determined mother. When Matthew began his military service his parents became angry, and did not encourage his travel and lengthy adventures. Their actions created a pain, a pain of loss and resistance. And so, Matthew took orders for lengthy navigational expeditions, he rarely returned to his homeland.

As his betrothal date grew near, he found himself at sea most of the year, and Althea's family had become a second family to him. He had known her brothers in their naval training; they had instantly become good acquaintances.

Their friendship brought him to the beautiful coastal village and to the heart of Althea's family. Indeed, the city had become his refuge. He loved the captivating harbor and village as well the De Savior Family, Jon Paul and his kin. It too was his sanctuary, like Ginevra.

His ties to Althea's family would forever bond him to this land. A new light seemed to shine in his heart. He fell in love with Althea but with guarded interest. In his mind, he knew his family continued to demand he follow through with his own marriage betrothal for the acquisition of a higher status and prestige for them. He knew the time had arrived to inform his family of the new love in his life, and break the betrothal.

Matthew also loved the comradeship he experienced from this bustling city. He docked his grand ship in the gentle harbor often as possible. He spent a great deal of time at the Hungry Traveler, (the Inn of the Jon Paul and his family). Here he could share stories and learn of the war that had invaded Europe. His contribution in the lively discussions of trade, politics, and social issues inspired his kindred spirit. Matthew's navigation skills and experience interested all that visited the busy tavern. Matthew was charting new sea courses, and the thrill of adventure intrigued all who listened.

Matthew docked his ship in the harbor as often as possible, even when he had the opportunity to return to Scotland...to his family. He treasured the time spent in this charming city, but most of all, he shared a growing fascination for Althea, of which she was not aware of until now. In Althea's mind, Matthew had seemed more like a brother and a friend, until she noticed her own gazes lingering on the horizon, searching for his arrival or inquiring of his travels.

Jon Paul was aware of this growing fascination and was pleased. They seemed most suited for one another. Both had sensitivity and were full of passion. Althea's father began to find ways to allow them to spend time together. It was then, their friendship began to blossom and strangely enough the beginning of one of Europe's most devastating and wicked wars of all time. "The Thirty Years War. The news of its spawning had reached the city, and all were concerned. One day, as Matthew sat at the old tavern, Jon Paul said "You must promise me this, son: if something happens to me—to us, Althea's family—you will please watch over her."

Matthew looked into the eyes of Jon Paul and replied gently, "Do not worry. You are all safe, and Althea will always be in the corner of my eye. I have grown quite fond of her and your family, Jon Paul. Have no fear, for I shall always be here."

Jon Paul was greatly relieved and replied with a strong salute. "To this Scotsman, may he live long and travel safely!"

Matthew felt honored and warranted in his intentions; this was the key to his own request. Matthew trusted this family, and they trusted him. Here was the love and future of his life—his family. He was fond of all, but his love for Althea had been reciprocated and her family approved. Now he knew with whom his future would be shared.

With reservation and apprehension, Matthew knew that he'd have to return to Scotland and take care of the family and military obligations. Matthew held his family in high esteem and had devoted himself to his country but the thought of the arranged betrothal angered him and always made him feel like an outsider, but indeed it was upon his plate and he would have to take care of it. He had escaped into a military and political career to relieve himself of the demands of his family. The dreams he had to be a sea captain and navigate the mysterious oceans and create maps were fulfilled, but he was still obligated to marry a woman of a prestigious family. Matthew did not know her and did not want to know her. His family only wanted the marriage to benefit the political standing of his own family. He was finally ready to make his voice be heard.

Althea was aware of Matthew's dilemma and encouraged him to live his life as he wished. She was fiercely independent and longed for her own dreams of writing and traveling. She told him, "Move forward, Matthew. Follow your dreams."

He admired her and found himself enamored by her beauty and essence and decided to return to his family at once. He would inform them of his adamant love for Althea and cancel the betrothal. He knew it was necessary to return the military ship. He was not happy to leave Althea and her family at this most uncertain time, but he would return quickly and with a clear mind.

On a gray and dismal morning, Matthew left the charming village. He bade a quick farewell to his friend Jon Paul with a sincere handshake and a promise that he would return shortly.

Jon Paul was aware of Matthew's apprehension and encouraged him to travel safely and return with a joyous heart. Jon Paul had also recognized Matthew's concern to take care of obligations to his family and his homeland of Scotland.

Matthew looked into Jon Paul's eyes and promised to return to Cote de Azur to fulfill his duty...to love and care for Althea throughout all time regardless of the troubled times. For he was certain that Althea and her family were already a part of his.

Althea watched Matthew, from the window of her stately villa, where the red bougainvillea draped its magnificence over the veranda, all overlooking the harbor. Her heart had gone heavy, and silent tears fell from her dark, restless eyes. She watched this man—the man who would rule her heart—leave her without a farewell. In her heart, she knew Matthew was thinking only of her, but he was not one to formally say good-bye. Earlier that week, Matthew had informed her of his responsibility to return to his family to take care of the necessary duties. He had finally confided in her, showing trust and confidence. He needed to return briefly to England and then a very necessary trip to Scotland...

Althea knew something important had to be taken care of. She trusted him, she loved him, and with that she knew he'd be gone for a short amount of time. Their love was on a course...

She watched how quietly he commanded his obedient crew, not demanding, but always working beside them, working as they. He was a part of a team and his team worked as a successful unit. Althea observed the event from her balcony and watched reverently...she saw a dedicated crew follow his lead, but she knew in her heart and by their actions they were not eager to leave, something had impaired their ambition, and that was obvious in their preparations to journey forth.

She spotted them looking her way, with apprehension and uncertainty. They followed their captain and indeed Althea knew that he not only commanded her heart, but the heart of those that followed him. A hushed silence fell upon all who boarded the ship.

Matthew looked out at the water, the sea was quiet and the water was smooth, but the sky looked ominous, dark and forbidding. A great storm was brewing, the clouds in the distance warned him... Matthew proceeded, but with with ample caution. He commanded the ship forward. His plan to journey first to England to deliver his irreplaceable maps, and then on to Scotland to complete his goal. And so, with the look of a commanding officer, Matthew signaled for departure from the quiet pristine harbor.

The *Scottish Queen* moved rapidly through the dark Atlantic.

Matthew's heart was heavy as he looked back at the beautiful village. His felt strangely torn, and in a whisper he heard the voice of his love in the cool wind. "Move forward, my love. I will wait for you." Matthew smiled despite his apprehension. His love for Althea had given him the courage to take care of this task that had plagued him with doubt and a lifetime of trouble with his family standing.

Matthew informed his crew of their duties and insisted that if anything should happen to him, they must return to France and fetch Althea and her family. They looked into his eyes and replied, "Indeed, we will always follow your command.

Chapter 2: Matthew Sails to England

*T*he regal ship moved slowly through the churning Atlantic Ocean. Time seemed suspended; the only movement was the ocean waves propelling the Scottish Queen forward. The sound of the wind beating against the great sails choired with the slapping of the waves against the vessel. The air was bitter, and the sky remained eerily grey and heavy with moisture. A floating mist filled the air, along with the beginnings of a tempest wind. There were no voices, just the steady crash of the waves moving the ship forward, away from Althea. Matthew thought carefully, "I will deliver the goods and the navigational maps as requested earlier by his military superiors. He was dedicated soldier, an officer, and a determined son; he would return the maps to the English authorities, and then without rest, journey to Scotland.

Little did he and his crew know that this voyage to England would prove to be a disaster. All sailors are at the whim of the sea, a strange and unpredictable change of events could always occur.

As the ship moved deeper into the sea, the sky began to darken, and the wind began to create great waves, huge swells, rising and falling, carelessly tossing the vessel about as if it were but a grain of sand in a swirling storm of dust. Daggers of lightening shocked the sky as the ship was lighted and brought close to electric sparks of fire. The sudden jolts of light shocked the dark sky bringing strange visions and ominous shadows. Matthew and the crew had never seen quite the storm and they fought gallantly to control the ship heeding the challenge like soldiers of the cross.

Arriving sadly in the dreary English harbor, and with a great deal of damage, the ship was finally moored indefinitely in its spot. Matthew and the crew said many quiet blessings as no one had perished even though the ship was mangled and brutally injured. It would eventually be repaired to its original condition, but because of the damage, Matthew was unable to go on to Scotland as quickly as he had planned. The extensive damage to the Scottish Queen required time consuming repair, the special parts, many broken beyond repair, were only created in Ireland and they would have to be delivered, which could take weeks or even months.

After two days in the English harbor, Matthew faced his greatest nightmare—it was rumored that many villages in France had suffered looting and pillaging from the true savages of this unyielding war. Because the coastal cities were vulnerable, they were hit the hardest. Matthew would not remain in England. He would leave at once!

With repairs modestly completed, parts of the vessel left broken, he and his crew took the Scottish Queen out into the sea again at full mast towards the troubled French seaside.

After long hours of persistent sailing, they rapidly approached the coastal city. Matthew again heard the wind calling him with the voice of Jon Paul. "Watch over her, lad. She will be there for you." With determination and force, Matthew had commanded the crew to move at full speed, twenty knots, toward the coastal village. Their arrival was quickly expedited by good weather and determination. And to the surprise of all, the vessel sailed as if nothing had been damaged, a strange and wonderful miracle.

Matthew was concerned about the possibility of war and the devastation that could follow, so he had pushed them rapidly forward, taking little time to rest or nourish their fatigued bodies.

As they approached the once-charming and pristine French harbor, a dark cloud full of pungent smoke filled the sky and warned them of the danger ahead. They inhaled this deathly smoke, which brought tears and fears to their ocean clear eyes.

Matthew and his crew worked rapidly to anchor the ship and move on to the feared destruction. They were silent and anticipated the worst. The smell of smoke and the ghastly odor of death filled their lungs with a frightening sense of doom. As they ran toward the village, the rubble and carnage was beyond Matthew's most vile dreams.

The little roads were strewn with small fires, broken wagons, burning buildings and...the carnage of the villagers... The silence of death loomed everywhere. The shops had been looted, doors broken from their hinges, and storefronts set on fire. Matthew ran toward the "Hungry

Traveler", afraid to look upon the dead that lay in his path. When he reached the tavern, he found it strangely, as he'd left it, empty though, but safe, quiet, and secure.

"Odd," Matthew whispered. "Why would this tavern be left untouched? It's as if it was protected by something or someone." Matthew entered and shouted, "Are you here, Jon Paul?" With no response, Matthew left the tavern, and frantically raced up the hill to the old villa of Jon Paul. It was nestled above the village, lined between the tall, once-green cypress trees now smoking and charred.

As Matthew approached the damaged villa, he felt as if his heart would stop beating. The elegant stone home was now a ruined outline of what was once a jewel of a home. With tears in his eyes, he backed away, pain shot threw his body... as he discovered what was left of Althea's parents.

Matthew fell to the ground, knowing he could do nothing. All had been destroyed. The horror of the scene was worse than any nightmare; other unknown bodies were scattered about—some were burned, others beaten and decapitated, but not one was left alive. Despite the horror of the gruesome scene, Matthew searched frantically to find Althea. Tears filled his handsome eyes. His crew also inspected the horrid scene, unable to find Althea's body. Matthew knew all was lost and felt unable to function, as his heart could not bear to see Althea.

***

In despair, Matthew again fell to his knees, and prayed to God to help him find his lady, somehow, somewhere...

His crew felt his pain, but with gentleness, they helped Matthew to his feet. Both deck hands realized that Matthew must be returned to the ship immediately, they had heard the sounds of battle in the far distance, if the looters returned, their own safety could be threatened. As they scanned the area, they saw familiar bodies and felt the horror of war pound through their veins. They searched and searched for Althea...she was not there.

They moved Matthew through the burning village, moving awkwardly upon the stone road filled with the blood and fires of war.

Matthew was muttering. He had gone into a strange consciousness. He kept saying over and over again, "She will be there; she will be there." The frightened sailors only wanted to return to their ship, but as they passed the old tavern, they also heard the voice of Jon Paul. "She is there. She is there. Go to her, take her with you."

Immediately Matthew seemed to awaken from his shock. He signaled to his crew to enter the old tavern. Strangely enough, even when the other shops were burned and looted, the small tavern remained unchanged as if angels had guarded the door of Jon Paul's Hungry Tavern.

The door of the tavern was ajar, and the three forlorn sailors entered cautiously. The tavern seemed cool and fresh, despite the burning of the other buildings, as if heaven had marked this establishment as sacred and pure. Matthew walked slowly to the familiar wooden bar, built of cypress from a salvaged, old, shipwrecked vessel; it was rugged but well cared for. His thoughts were of Jon Paul, and how the old bar reminded him of the good man. As a tear rolled down his handsome face, he heard a soft whimpering. As if powered by an unknown force, he walked to the rear corner of the cool tavern, a corner partitioned by a cloth Althea had draped for her privacy. She had worked here, writing or studying. This was a place she called hers, among the crowds and the noise of the busy tavern. "Of all places," Matthew remembered. "Could she not have found a quiet and scenic spot outdoors where she could be away from the noise and chaos?"

As he approached this most memorable spot, a gentle sound of breathing and a fresh ocean breeze filled him with recognition. There, before him, Althea rested on the small wooden cot. The cool breeze seemed to have pushed him to her. She was unafraid, but seemed lost in a strange type of consciousness, neither asleep nor awake. He looked into her vacant brown eyes and she sighed with a vacant stare. She was despondent but very much alive. Shivering with cold, despite the heat of the fire charred night, she reached for him. Matthew took her hand, talked to her gently, but Althea remained silent. She took his hand and rose, and as she did, her consciousness left her, and she collapsed into his arms.

Matthew walked silently, with Althea safely embraced within his arms, gesturing to his mates to follow. They whisked her away, returning at once to the moored *Scottish Queen*, waiting to take him and his crew away from this sad and horrible nightmare.

Quickly the crew, Althea in Matthew's arms boarded the small boat that would take them to the Scottish Queen. As they rowed through the dark water of the harbor, they saw abandoned fishing boats floating through the eerie, smoke-darkened lagoon. The setting sun tried to shine through the clouds of gray smoke, but only small rays of light managed to escape the dark clouds, as if heaven had found a way to light the darkness, to give a promise. As one dancing ray of light emerged, a small, floating seashell twinkled and caught Matthew's eye. He reached down and grasped the pretty pink shell and put it in Althea's cold hand. She instantly recognized its beauty, and tears began to stream from her dark eyes. In French, Althea spoke eloquently, "I will be strong, and I will carry the spirit of my village within my heart and soul." Matthew gently comforted her and stroked her tear-stained cheek.

Chapter 3: Matthew and Althea Sail to Ireland

After the *Scottish Queen* departed the smoky harbor and began its voyage north to the Emerald Isle, Matthew carried Althea's wilted body to his private quarters below deck. Here she would be quiet and free from the horrors of war. He could watch over her, and care for her. He would try to help her regain her composure. He placed her gently upon the bed, her pretty face covered with dried tears and bits of ashes.

As he placed her carefully upon the soft bed he noticed the delicate cameo necklace hanging on Althea's slender neck. It was the one her mother had always worn. It was made of the pink shells found on the Cote de Azur shoreline. Despite her desperation, her beauty shone like a morning ray of light, the cameo too, reflecting the same warm radiance.

He carefully covered her limp body with an old Scottish tartan with the field of blue and green stripes. The heart and courage of his Viking blood would watch over her. He began to wonder what she had seen or experienced during the slaughter of the village. Even though she was despondent and frightened, she had been left untouched—her clothing, hair, and skin were as pretty as the day he had met her. She displayed no signs of injury or physical pain. *How did she stay out of harm's way?* Matthew thought. His prayers had been answered and his bond with God gave him the strength to continue his endeavors.

Althea had been so scared and upset that Matthew assumed that she had suffered from the violent attack, and indeed she had, but her body was undisturbed, as if she too, like the old tavern, had been protected. With the hope of her recovery, Matthew began to again remember the devastation. He had seen some battles in his life, but never had he experienced the unfathomable events that must have occurred. He knew the war had been brewing for quite some time, but to actually see the aftermath of such violence and anger directed at a village of innocents—only trying to remain neutral, just trying to care for their young—caused Matthew's soul to fire torments to the ones responsible for such violence.

His greatest concern was Althea's welfare. He had no idea what she had experienced. Again, he observed and in his amazement Matthew thought, "She did not appear to be injured or violated in any way. She did not even smell of smoke; she was fresh and clean, like a new day. But indeed, she had suffered. She was quivering as if her body was cold, but her brow was damp with perspiration. She was frightened and withdrawn. She acknowledged him but did not seem to recognize his face; she had a vacant look, as if she had left something behind." And indeed she had...she had lost her world, her mother, her father, her home, her joy. Matthew's eyes clouded with tears and his heart missed a beat, for he too suffered. He also loved the De Savior family...as his own. He loved the village, the villagers...

With gentle words, Matthew tried to regain Althea's mind. "My love, are you all right? Please talk to me, Althea." He waited and then released her. Matthew looked into her eyes and saw her fear and also her gratefulness for his returning to help her as her father had asked. Though no words came from her shaking lips, Matthew heard her speak through her gentle soft eyes, and at once, he knew she would be all right. "For lovers need not question but only listen. The voice of mysterious empirical knowledge sought forth."

Althea's breathing was shallow almost faint, Matthew spoke to her gently, "My darling Althea, you must rest. Please close your eyes. I will return with some food, but my love, you must know you are safe, and I will be here for you, today and forever. I love you, my sweet, beautiful woman. We will soon be far away and live where your heart will again beat with love and happiness." As Matthew spoke, he caressed her honey-blonde hair that was as fine as the silk from China.

Althea began to relax and fell into a deep sleep. Matthew sat with her for several hours, watching over her gently, like the sleeping babe in its warm bed.

As he watched her, he too felt weary and closed his eyes. He fell into a turbulent sleep, hoping for a promise of better days.

Later that evening, Matthew returned to the upper deck of his steadfast ship, watching the night skies as they illuminated with a galaxy of sparkling stars. He watched the restless sea as it pushed the casted sails of the ship to a distant shore.

Here, Matthew was always able to think and make a preparation for the next day. His thoughts were drifting to the north, and as the ship cruised through the smooth Atlantic, making its pitch forward, Matthew knew that he too must move forward. His concern for Althea was his ambition...an attribute of all good men, listening to the powerful guide of love, devotion, and duty.

Althea was safe and would remain that way. His plan was to take her to the northern part of Ireland to his family's summer home, an isolated old castle that sat close to the sea. The castle was minimally staffed but always ready for he and his family.

There, Althea could stay in the safety of the grand fortress for as long as she wanted—as long as they wanted. This would be their home and their children's home. They would live well and prosper.

The castle was perched high on the Irish Cliffs of Moher; it was actually an old refuge of early Christians and Viking warriors. Matthew and his family had cherished their time here. He and his family had lived here many a summer, and his fond memories rekindled the sense of adventure, when he and his siblings played along the coast and explored the mysterious caves. Matthew and one of his younger brothers had once thought they had spotted a beautiful mermaid resting on the rocks in a beautiful cove, haunted by the dead sailors that had perished in the dark waters. The legend stated the mermaids lived in this deep watered cove to remain by the side of their cherished sailors, and here they would remain to the end of time.

Matthew remembered her vividly—long hair tossed and gently spilling down her back, ending in childlike curls. Her fresh skin and fish-scaled body shimmered in the bright Irish sun, but she looked heartbroken, as though she were missing someone. He laughed at himself, feeling both delighted and inspired. This memory was strange and mysterious. Matthew always doubted it, even as he knew it to be true, as the sightings were numerous and not just by him but by others, who had also questioned the authenticity of the mermaid. It was known that many lonely sailors had spotted the beautiful mermaids, who seemingly coaxed the sailors into the dark, cold waters.

His family clan was a line of very ancient Swedish ancestors who had traveled to Scotland, and there they battled their way to success and prosperity, becoming one of the oldest and most victorious people of the Scottish; his immediate family was a total of eight vivacious and proud Scotsmen. Because of their prosperity, they had been educated and had succeeded to the royal line of Scottish ancestry. His memories of this beautiful dwelling lifted his dark mood, and he began to make a plan for the future for his new family.

Again, he would have to leave Althea and complete this unfinished business in Scotland. He could never move on until he fulfilled his duty as an officer, soldier and a loving son bent by his obligations. His heart would rule, but he would also complete his sworn duties.

As the Scottish Queen moved quickly to the near shores of Ireland he began to plan his future departure. He knew the journey to Scotland from Ireland was a short in distance. He would be away shortly and return with the future in his hand and his family in his heart.

He knew Althea would be safe with the staff at Delany Castle. Althea needed to rest and his staff would take fine care of her. He was as fond of them as his own kin. He had known them most of his life. They were distant cousins, and he trusted them because they had lived in the castle with the family for two generations. Delany Castle been built for families and that was his ultimate plan—to fill the castle with his and Althea's children and attend to his duties of navigation, trade, and commerce. The importation of goods to the small village below the castle would follow. The village had been created from the economy of the castle, and those that inhabited the quiet village were like another family. Together they prospered, as their children would also.

After his brief visit to Scotland, he would return shortly and their life would continue, and this time without a troubled mind. His spirit would be free to live happily, now and forever...

Matthew's mind began racing...He thought passionately, "Althea needed to rest and recover from the tragedy of Cote de Azur, the loss of her family and her village". He was aware that women sometimes needed the tending of other women. She would be well, and he would conquer his personal battles..."

The rising mist of early night began to cloud his eyes, and the damp chill in the ocean air reminded him of the fragile Althea left in his quarters. He knew he must take her food and drink, and he hoped she would converse with him. He was aware that she was in distress and needed to rest. He had no idea how long it had been since she had eaten. She had slept many hours and would need to sleep again, but for now, he would fetch some broth and bread, all contained in the small galley below the deck.

As Matthew stepped quickly to the lower deck, he began to feel the hope of his future plans. The devastation of the French village had taken a tremendous toll on his spirit, and he felt responsible for preparing his own family and country for the epidemic of war. In the warm galley, he placed several items on a familiar silver tray, with the symbol of his clan stamped within a center circle. Matthew knew his family had dedicated their lives to the throne and would remain a long legend. This crest was meaningful to him, but love was more important than royalty; he felt a gentle pang in his kind heart. On this tray, above the crest, they would enjoy their first meal as a family.

Bringing his mind to a rational thought, Matthew also knew that he must inform Althea of his obligation to return to Scotland. He would ask her to marry him and tell her of his plans for them to live happily in Delany Castle. He realized this would trouble Althea, but she would understand and honor him for his determination to resist the unwanted promise that he had made to his family. His only dream was to love Althea and their future children and the challenge of navigation of the mysterious, dark uncharted oceans.

As he ascended the galley and moved forward to his quarters, he heard the cries and tortured screams of Althea. With a sense of urgency, he quickly set the silver tray on a table and rushed to Althea. Her voice was not of the Althea he had known, and it frightened him.

At last, when he came to her, she was in a restless sleep, tossing about upon the heirloom tartan blanket. Her eyes were rolling, and she began to exhibit a type of nightmare. Immediately, he comforted her, not knowing what to do or say. Her shouts and screams were of a torment that moved through her possessed body. He called her name, and when she opened her eyes, he saw that they were blood red. In perfect French she pleaded for him to stay near and not to ever leave. Her body was clammy, and perspiration rolled over her delicately arched brows.

Matthew grabbed her forcefully, trying to keep her from falling. At once, she shouted loudly "The walls are cold! Your heart is frozen!" He tried to calm her, but to no avail. Althea's body seemed violent and strangely powerful. Her breathing and her odd voice frightened him. She defied his embrace and desperately tried to set herself free. Finally, in desperation, Matthew held her and began to murmur an old Scottish prayer.

Instantly, she grasped him with a powerful pull. For what seemed forever, Matthew waited for her breathing to relax and her mind to quiet. Slowly, his beautiful maiden began to soften, returning to the spirit of the princess that she truly was. With tears in his eyes, this enchanted embrace gave way to a kiss of love and passion, a never-ending kiss.

Althea's tears flowed onto Matthew's face. Feeling her fear and astonished with his own fear, he vowed to honor her, and there they slept until the night skies lightened to welcome a new day.

The ship moved rapidly through the smooth, rolling sea, as if joyful and ready to harbor in the Irish port.

When Althea awoke, she was not shaking or even frightened. She had once again returned to her state of grace, but her eyes were sorrowful, low and mourning for her lost family. Matthew comforted her, and she returned his warmth. They were now at peace, and the "spell" had been lifted.

He was pleased to see her looking again like herself—and strangely so, as if a gentle spirit had filled her with a peace and contentment. Together, they breakfasted and began a quiet conversation about the ship.

Althea revealed, to Matthew's delight, she had a passion for the antique sailing vessel and wanted to know everything about its splendor. In a gentle plea, Althea asked Matthew to show her the vessel. She said, in a new and enthusiastic voice, "My love, please give me a tour through this ship."

Matthew was pleased to hear Althea speak with such enthusiasm and clarity. He replied calmly and gently, "Althea, I will show you this old and sacred vessel" When her brown eyes again twinkled, he became filled with an unfathomable love, she had overcome her darkest nightmare, he thought joyously.

She replied, "When will I see her?"

Matthew said without hesitation, "At once!" That familiar twinkle had indeed returned to Althea's dark eyes, speckled with glints of gold. Althea was filled with love and an enthusiasm for this grand ship. Matthew began to tell of the regal ship, "This vessel was built by the Irish and was christened to be a ship bound not for war, as most military ships, but instead for peace and prosperity. It was built to be used for expeditions and exploration...the discoveries of new lands and the makings of charts and maps to return to these uncharted territories."

As Althea toured the vessel, she was reminded of her loving and gentle brothers, so far away. Althea was silent, riveted with a fond memory. When Matthew asked Althea why she smiled so warmly, she exclaimed, "Matthew, my brothers also sail, and I believe we will soon find them."

Matthew smiled at her and replied, "Ah, yes, we will find those lads sailing the seas with great vivacity and determination."

Matthew knew this was an opportunity to acquaint Althea with his need to return to Scotland...so that he could inform his family of his dedication to her. Matthew began, "Althea, my beauty, I have many obligations. I have military duties, and I must report my findings as a navigating sea captain to my commanding officers. Furthermore, I must return briefly to my clan, my family to tell them of my... our great love."

It was at that moment that Althea's face saddened as she anticipated his departure. He gazed lovingly into her warm brown eyes and then gently asked her, "Will you— my goddess, my love, my life, and the future mother of my babes—honor me by allowing me to join you as your husband for now and forever more?"

Althea smiled again and bowed her head. "We already are, my sacred love of days gone by, for we are married by God through our eternal love." Matthew smiled at her and her independent spirit with great passion and determination. He told her that he would love her forever and always, upon one and all distant shores. She nestled her head on his shoulder, and the two became a figure of one, a sculpture of love and fortitude...but silently a tear the size of a rare and hopeful diamond rolled down her face...

By means of a warm heart and a future plan, they ascended the royal quarters and returned to the upper deck of the wooden vessel, with souls deeper than the mighty dark blue of the Atlantic. As they journeyed to the upper deck, they encountered a mysterious fog floating gently upon the ship. Althea and Matthew walked through the fog, and as they did, tiny sparkles of light seemed to emanate from it. Althea tilted her head back, trying to embrace the sacred moment, "They were together...all, and here God had looked upon them and blessed their love. Matthew kissed her lovely white neck. In seconds, the sun began to cast its warm embrace around the ship and warmed the hearts of all who traveled on the ship.

With a new and fresh demeanor, they began to tour the *Scottish Queen*. Althea was eager to see her surroundings, and Matthew was proud to show her and pleased that she seemed so well. Even the deck hands were amazed to see her looking so recovered and lovely. She smiled at them tenderly and stated with a sweet and assertive command, "Full mast, mates!" And with astonishment, they nodded their respectful heads and responded, "My lady, we shall do!" And with gusto, they released the sails, and an unexpected gale traveled to the ship and sent it quickly through the sparkling blue ocean.

Althea was radiant, despite the darkness of the morning mist. Dawn was lifting its somber head with the rays of pink sunshine. "Red skies in the morning, a sailor's warning," one of the bold crew shouted out. There were a few patchy places in the cloudy sky, where small, rosy rays of sunlight filtered through the dark clouds and miraculously, above the loving couple, an arc of many colors showed itself—a bright rainbow. As the deck hands became aware, they felt a true joy and sense of hope, despite the sailor's warning. Happiness seemed to infiltrate their hearts, forfeiting the old ancestor's myth of morning warnings. The waves seemed calmer, and the gentle wind whisked them forward, as if the breath of God was pushing them a little faster and a little safer to the emerald-green isle of Ireland.

Later as morning faded into a cool afternoon and the afternoon crowned its glory to evening, Matthew sat on the deck of the *Queen*. He was deep in thought and had little to declare. His heart was torn. He watched the orange ball of light sink slowly into the horizon.

His thoughts were drifting to the dark northern skies. On the Irish island, Althea would be safe, he reassured himself. He would return rapidly from his homeland, Scotland, to make sure she would remain so. He and Althea would live happily and safely in the family castle.

He had not returned to the old fortress since it had been completely renovated.

All renovation was to be done with the Scottish style of his mother's clan, and no expense would be too grand for this elegant summer palace. The castle was visible from the sea, and one could easily gaze across the entire coastline, seeing all who voyaged near to the green isle. Here, Althea could stay, protectively guarded by the grand fortress. Just as the castle had been a refuge of early Christians and Viking soldiers, so would it be for Althea. She would have everything she ever needed or wanted.

Matthew's family was an educated and regal group, with true warrior blood. They were given ownership of the castle after a clash of swords, for this was their God-given land, and their sovereignty would forever live on. His memories lifted his dark mood, even as he thought of his impending plan. He had much to accomplish and then he would return to Althea, to live a long and cherished life. Dunlance Castle was their life, and there they would live forever. His only ambition, forgetting to embrace the sacred moment, living in the moment, and not the moment in which they would not.

Chapter 4: Matthew and Althea Arrive in Ireland

*T*he captain's deck hands exploded with joyful voices, calling out "Land ho!" Matthew and Althea awakened with a start, dressed quickly, and emerged from their warm lair to see the land that would give refuge to their children. They prepared for their departure, the ship they had called their sanctuary with a sense of joy and sadness. They gathered a few items, and left for the island of Atrial. As they climbed to the open deck, Althea's eyes spanned the rugged coastline and the grand cliffs. With zest and inspiration, she grabbed Matthew's cloak, and kissed him, and shouted, "*Vive le emerald de isles!*" Her voice was feeble but held a determined, rebellious tribute.

Matthew smiled at her. She had such an oddly innocent way of expressing her passion. Althea could feel the history of Ireland, which presented itself differently, yet she felt a growing love for it deep within her heart and her mind. She thought with great passion, *This land is rugged, old, and holds a mysterious air of royalty.* Here, she could feel the echoes of history and the beam of the future. "Oh, her grand skies and rich green hills, surrounded by the deep, mysterious ocean, always rolling, bringing stories of love and enchantment ..."

Althea felt at peace here. She heard the ancients' voice of evermore, reciting, "Go forth, Althea. Raise your young and remember our voices!" As if she were guided by an inner compass, she boldly took in the beauty and the spirit of the land and its ancestors within her heart and soul.

The brisk air and the majestic scenery pleased her. She knew of Matthew's life, and he beamed with pride and elation. Matthew commented to Althea, "Look into the distant horizon, my love. There is our dwelling. Here, we will abide with our children until the end of time."

Althea focused on the castle, small in the distance. Her gentle eyes filled with tears, and she whispered to Matthew, "Come what will be, you are my love and my destiny."

With love and confidence, they walked, arms locked, to the small village, where they arranged transportation to Dunlance. Many villagers were eager to speak to Matthew and meet his lady love. Upon seeing the lord of their little island, they greeted Matthew jovially, "Ahieee, velcome, Lord MacDonnell. They gave him a Scottish kneel and grand salute. Matthew looked upon them with great honor. "I salute you from the shores of afar. I greet you and proudly present my honorable lady, Princess Althea of France, to the people and the shores of the mermaid coves of gentle land and sea, abundant of life and legend." With welcoming and warm bows, Althea was honored and immediately felt like a queen of a new and wondrous land. The islanders loved the MacDonnell clan, as they had brought prosperity and honor to their humble and quiet land. The islanders watched with utter amazement, as the welcomed couple moved, and a multicolored light began to glow above the pretty island—an arc of light. This arc seemed like a sign of never-ending hope. They recognized the beauty as a greeting from the highest of highs, as Noah saw above his wandering vessel in a world of water. "Thou shall live ever more." The islanders knew their arrival would bring greater prosperity and happiness to the village. And their Lord arriving with such a lady, caused their hopes to take them far into future prosperity. Matthew's warm smile thanked them for the welcome. He introduced Althea, as his fiancée. They were delighted and overjoyed with this fine news.

Matthew left Althea with a merchant at a small outdoor market, opened in the wee hours of the day. Matthew said to Althea, "My dearest, stay here, at this market. These fine people will assist you. Choose whatever you may need. I will return shortly with our mounts, and then we will journey to our home in the old cliffs above."

Althea was charmed and smiled. "Ah, my darling, leave me with no worry, for this good woman will help me and guide me."

Matthew smiled warmly, as he was aware that she had left Cote de Azur with nothing but the dress she was wearing on that horrible day when she had lost everything. He smiled as he thought of the morning when she decided to make a change in clothing—she had dressed in the fine plaid kilt that was hung in the ship's armoire. She had looked quite dapper in the kilt and the regalia as she had emerged from the cabin with the elegance of a top-ranking Scottish officer. The green-and-black plaid had suited her olive skin and light blonde hair. Her dark eyes seemed darker and emphasized the black stripes within the tartan.

***

He remembered the look of happiness and humor in Althea's eyes when she stood before him in his clothes. She was playful, and he was very intrigued by her gesture.

After Matthew smiled and bowed to the clerk and owner of the store, he winked and a ray of warm sunlight beamed through his hair. The wise clerk smiled and knew there was a blessing around this grand couple.

Althea browsed through the goods. She found two pretty dresses—nothing fancy but practical, made of a soft woolen fabric embedded with a plaid of violet and rose. She found a silver hairbrush, a fresh undercoat for the cold Irish mornings, and a dark overcoat that would warm her on chilly evenings. She then found a pair of boots made with the softest leather and immediately put them on. The clerk smiled to see her so practical and so innocent. As the clerk handed her the wrapped parcel containing Althea's purchases, Althea smiled and her eyes twinkled.

As Althea walked to the door, a shining crystal caught her attention. It was transmitting a colorful reflection of a light spectrum—a rainbow, just like the one over the ship. She was overjoyed with something so unique. As she followed the colorful beams of light, she found two soft woolen blankets made with the fleece of lambs, each edged with a ribbon.

Althea was overwhelmed with joy, and tears gently rolled down her face. It was at this moment, she knew the future. The clerk saw this and was filled with the love and joy of a bountiful future. She said gently to the young French lady, "Is this your wish and your yearning?"

Althea replied with the gentleness of a warm spring morning, "With all my heart and my loving family blood, it is." A silent lullaby seemed to fill the pretty shop, along with a fragrance of lilac and French lavender. She felt a strange and sweet movement within her delicate body. With elegance and innocence, Althea smiled and thanked her profoundly in eloquent French. The clerk, in astonishment, saw a warm circle of light around Althea's head. Without knowledge of the light, Althea smiled down at the parcel. This radiating ring of light gently circled her head with holy glows of inner peace and created a masterpiece of love's true light, as given upon this great and wondrous land.

The parcel was bulky, and Althea balanced it on her hip. At that moment, Matthew breezed into the small shopping stall, eager to return to his fine home with his lady by his side. But, upon viewing Althea slightly hunched over and in tears, he stopped. Her actions were many times odd and unusual, lacking the conventional grace that many ladies thought they could acquire. He had always been fascinated by her, even in the tavern and along the sandy shore of her village. She would occasionally sit and seem to be in a trance, sometimes speaking words of wisdom unknown to him. Then she would look away and then at him, completely coherent, as if she was unaware of her unusual actions.

When Matthew saw Althea slightly hunched over, with a large wrapped parcel at her waist, she looked as round as a woman with child. As he approached her, he looked down at her long slim fingers. She was holding two woven baby blankets laced with ribbons. A soft multicolored light seemed to shine over them and through Althea's fingers. Matthew was astonished when he saw teardrops glistening on each ribbon, reflecting a strong ray of light on his face. At that moment, Matthew also heard the sound of babes, and his face gleamed. Both were suspended in time, and a moment later, they joined hands and left the store. The clerk, who had witnessed the fascinating events, proceeded to wrap the delicate blankets.

She was a wise Irish woman, with an inkling for the good fortune of all. She knew the happy pair shared a wonderful moment that was well worth remembering. In time, she would have the blankets delivered to the castle. She had knitted them only last week, all done with the wool she had spun from her first small herd of lambs. *How odd,* she thought, *the blankets, each damp with the fallen teardrops.* Her thoughts went wild with the idea that these blankets would each have one precious baby—twins! *God shined down on these fine young people,* she thought. The shopkeeper went about her work with a newfound happiness and an extra kick in her walk. She placed the blankets in a basket to be delivered to the master's castle—but not too soon, as their marriage had not been announced; their love preceded that. The old Irish shopkeeper was longing to see and hear all new arrivals, be they young or old, all bringing life and commerce to the Emerald Isle.

Matthew and Althea mounted the borrowed horses from a nearby farm. They were for the journey to Delany Castle. Matthew watched Althea with concern, but she was already astride, stroking the liver chestnut mare, which seemed eager to travel the twisting and rugged road to Delany. Mathew was not aware of Althea's equestrian skills, as few horses roamed the French coast. To his dismay and fascination Althea mounted the liver chestnut horse gracefully and took the leather reins into her hands as though she had done so a million times.

To his astonishment she appeared comfortable astride this spirited steed. And indeed, Althea was eager to ride. Mounting a horse was strangely familiar, yet never had she done so.

Matthew was still amazed by the events that had occurred at the village shop. Althea was unshaken by all the events and looked like a queen returning to her castle.

The road was rough and rocky, but it was not steep. The climb to the castle was strenuous for the horses, but they had done this many times and did not mind their labor. Matthew saw the gleam in Althea's eyes as she diligently guided her horse to its destination. This was a route that she would have to take occasionally. Matthew wanted to make sure she was knowledgeable and able. Matthew asked her, "Will you remember this path, my love?"

She smiled and replied, "Not only will I remember it, but I will savor it as my first task to arrive at my destiny."

Matthew stated clearly, "There is another road, longer and less steep, specifically made for the wagons. This was created during the construction of the castle." Althea looked at Matthew and only charged forward. Her actions said more than words could ever mean. They did not speak most of the way, except for a few gentle comments about the path ahead. Matthew's mind took him to the beginning of his future family. Would they soon have children? His hopes were clear, but he was adamant about the marriage and Althea's honor. She had aroused a great passion, but he had shown restraint, making sure she was not disturbed before their spiritual union. Althea did not seem concerned for this traditional custom. She had stated, "In God's eyes, we are one, because our love has endured the many tribulations of life."

The strange occurrence in the shop was a vision, Matthew knew of visions, but he was skeptical and dismissed the idea. Their journey continued at a rapid rate, and Althea asked Matthew to please stop so the horses could rest.

She also patted her pretty belly, or so it seemed. Matthew was never sure of this magnificent woman, so strong and so unusual. Her actions were always mysterious and playful. He motioned her to follow him, and to her amazement, they arrived at a freshwater spring, fed by high flowing waterfall. Its beauty was spectacular. The roaring crystal water fell from over two hundred feet of hard granite. The falls created a mist of diamond drops of water, sparkling and cooling the warm green earth.

Althea's gaze was of great appreciation. She lifted her head, inhaled the memory, and waited for the piercing drops of water to cool her warm face, pink from the warm sun and the labor of the ride. When Matthew looked at her, he was touched by her beauty and her spirit. The aesthetic value would forever remain in his memory.

Althea shouted with jubilation, "This is a place of my dreams! I would love to visit the beautiful falls or even spend time writing here."

"Ah, my love, this is yours—this land, this water, and this day. It is yours to visit any time you have the need," Matthew replied nobly. The day had warmed, and the sun was high in the Irish sky. The horses had worked up a good lather. As Matthew hobbled both horses carefully. He looked up when he heard a squeal of delight and the splashing of water.

The area was quite secluded, but the sun shone its light upon the water that twinkled like a diamond. There before him was his lady love in nothing but her olive-toned Mediterranean skin. Matthew was fascinated with Althea's beauty and her innocent joy. She was completely at ease with her nudity. He called to her, "You are more splendid than the angels from above!" She laughed and threw him a loving kiss. She climbed the rocks to a high place, and in an instant, he watched her dive gracefully into the deep pool. Although warm and eager to join her, he first watched with admiration and love. He disrobed and quickly made his way into the water. The water was cool, and instantly Matthew's warm body was refreshed.

His childhood memories returned and he imagined he was swimming to his lovely mermaid. As they frolicked, he laughed with Althea and told her of the days of his childhood, when he and his siblings would hike to this very place. They would swim and rest themselves often, even on the cool days. This place reminded him of his family, and for the first time in years, he felt sentimental about his kin.

Althea asked him boldly, "Why are you so distant to them? They love you and only want you to be happy."

Matthew knew in his heart she was right and immediately felt closer to her than ever. He reached out to her, feeling his passion stir deep within. As he approached her, the current in the water began to stir and gently push them into an enchanted embrace. Here, they embraced like lovers and found the love that existed and would continue to exist. Like a fast, clever fish, Althea exited the pool to climb to the high rock. She showed no signs of modesty, and he took his time to examine her feminine form. Her legs were long and strong, her stomach flat but softly pouched. "Ah, my lassie is ripe for child." His Scottish roots and Viking warrior instincts began to rumble through his body. Her long, glossy hair made a lovely silhouette of her beautiful form. He had never seen her so confident and lovely. Again, she made another splash into the pool, and as she entered, she looked exactly like the mermaid he had observed as a child along the rocky shore of the isle. This vision left him in awe and bewilderment. She swam slowly to him.

Althea, whispering in French and delighting him, said, "Indeed, in this moment I must use my French, because the love and beauty I feel cannot be spoken in English." Matthew swam to her and gently kissed her soft, pink lips, as cold as the Irish night. They laughed and frolicked in the fresh water, reviving their senses and filling their bodies with the precious minerals contained within the spring water. They swam and floated, and their minds became one. Matthew swam to the shore of the elegant pool and warmed his magnificent body in the beaming sunlight. In eagerness, Althea climbed out of the pool and retired her cold body next to his warm, muscular frame. Matthew wrapped his strong arms around Althea. After a passionate embrace, they warmed their cool bodies and became forever united. The warm sun shone down upon them, and the mist in the air reflected the love they shared.

They rested and warmed their bodies on the mossy rock shoreline, and soon they drifted into a carefree sleep, embracing their love as one—a love that would last an eternity. Without their knowledge, the great sun of the Irish sky placed a memorable shadow on the rocks. This miraculous shadow displayed a familiar Irish symbol—the *claddagh*, which means stony shore. The shadow displayed a heart clasped with two hands and a crown over the heart. Directly above their bodies, this image displayed itself with clarity.

Both horses saw the vision and snorted in anticipation. The instincts of the equine were finely tuned and well worth noting. But this miracle was not left to only the fine horses; it was observed by a special person—someone not meaning to spy or casually catch the lovers in their intimate embrace. The lady caretaker, Eliza McCormick, Matthew's nanny and caretaker of the Delany Castle. She came upon the vision by surprise while she was collecting the rare truffles that grew near the falls. She had watched them in awe and was stunned by the sacred image the rocks portrayed. So astounded was she, that she returned to her grazing old cart horse and made way to the castle, as quickly and quietly as she could.

Althea awakened and walked to the spooked horses. She calmed them at once and stroked their fine coats. She was so alive and felt the stirring of life deep within her. These horses gave her spirit a feeling of luck and security, she would offer that to them as well.

Matthew smiled and said, "Ye, going home dressed like that, lassie?"

Althea turned around and boldly returned his joke. "Ah, and would you still love me if I did?" They joked with Irish humor as Althea opened the parcel containing her new clothing, a pair of breeches, and a fine Irish-wool dress. She dressed quickly, placed the fine leather boots on her slender feet, and brushed her beautiful hair. Her beauty was unstoppable. Matthew was proud and content. They took their time and allowed the horses to drink to their fill.

Matthew asked, "Are you happy, my love?" She smiled at him and replied with a poem, all recited in French. Matthew gazed lovingly and asked her to say the poem in English.

Althea replied, "In time, my love, you will read many poems, but this one is special, and it is for you and our harmonious future. At last, they mounted the rested horses and soon found themselves approaching the fortress that Althea had dreamed of, long before her days of life here on this enchanted island, so green and cool.

As they approached the MacDonnell Castle, Althea noted, "The meadows and hillsides were exceptionally quiet, except for the sound of the roaring and rolling Atlantic surf. There was the faint sound of seagulls squawking and small birds fluttering, catching insects and sucking sweet nectar from the many wildflowers growing randomly among the green grass and clover."

Matthew dismounted his lathered horse and looked up at Althea—she looked like his sacred Mary. He smiled and she returned his smile with a gentle sigh. He led the fatigued horses to the stable, and when they approached the covered paddock, a young lad grabbed the reins gently and exclaimed with a thick Irish accent, "I greet thee, Master Matthew, and 'tis my honorable pleasure, my lady. Allow me the honor to stable these fine animals."

Matthew smiled at the lad and gave him the reins. Althea also looked at the young boy and gave him a warm smile. She then reached into her brown parcel and passed the young lad a very new and sweet bit, a food meant for children. The boy looked at her with astonishment and bowed. She laughed and thanked him. Althea looked at Matthew and teased, "Master, eh? Fetch me my treasure and off with you!"

Matthew looked into her playful eyes and replied, "I shall take my treasure, my lady. Off that animal and into our manger!" She slid off the left side of the horse and fell into his arms. They kissed, and angels stirred.

Matthew heard a beckoning call from the back of the castle. "'Ello, I say, 'ello!" Matthew beamed a warm smile as Mrs. McCormick greeted them with a welcome. "So good to have you back master." she remarked genuinely.

Matthew immediately returned her congeniality, "And tis good to be back, yer face is as lovely as always Mrs. McCormick." Matthew noticed her smile was slightly guarded, and seemed a little frightened, so unlike her usual tough and loving self.

"Ah, hush now young man, you won't be getting ur way with that kind of flattery!"

Matthew snickered, "I see you haven't changed at all my good woman."

She looked at Althea and her eyes filled with awe and splendor, but concern and apprehension. This lass was not Irish, but she was a vision of loveliness and something mysterious beyond all pages of her good book. Formally, Matthew introduced Mrs. McCormick to his lady love. Althea was charming, smiled and embraced her and then gave the old woman a kiss on each cheek.

Mrs. McCormick smiled and bowed and quickly told them that supper would be served shortly. "Yes, we shall be there, Madam McCormick." Althea was pleased to see their rapport but questioned the coolness she felt from the dear woman.

Matthew sensed Althea's concern. He winked and pinched Althea gently on her modestly padded bottom. "Ah, I am your king, princess, and I am ordering you to join me for supper!" Again, they giggled, their rapport becoming one of fun and joviality.

As they entered the kitchen through the back of the castle, Althea took in the warmness of the room. A stone fireplace stood at the back of the kitchen; it glowed dimly. Plates and utensils had been placed around the table, and an ample supply of bread and other food had been set upon the long wooden table.

Even though Matthew had presented Mrs. McCormick to his future bride and the exchange had been warm and accepting, the two women exchanged a serious salutation. Matthew thought carefully, "What is this animosity? The female is never easy to comprehend...he was certain Mrs. McCormick disapproved, she would get over that!"

At once, Althea's face lit up at the sight of the claddagh ring on the woman's finger. "So very pretty!" stated Althea.

Mrs. McCormick looked staunchly into Matthew's eyes but said to Althea, "Yes indeed, and you shall have one soon, I assume." Matthew chuckled at her matronly assertiveness and gave her a long boyish hug.

Matthew declared, "Ah, what is this in me pocket? I was waiting for the perfect time to betroth my love. This is as fine a time as any." Matthew lowered himself to one knee and looked into the twinkling eyes of his love. "Will you, my lady, be so fine as to humble me, by allowing me to love you as I believe you also love me? Will you take me as your lawfully wedded husband from now to eternity?"

Althea also kneeled but with both knees to the floor and her head bowed. "Indeed I will, but you must promise to love your children as you love me, through all time and eternity."

Mrs. McCormick was overcome with joy. Tears began to fall like the waters from the nearby lake. Her staunch face lightened, and was covered with the last rays of sunshine beaming through the small window near the shelf. At the same moment, Mr. McCormick and little Sean entered the old kitchen and clapped their hands and danced with glee. They had overheard the announcement as they entered the kitchen.

They popped open a bottle of their best ale. All sipped the fine amber liquid and sat themselves down for a fitting meal, but before the meal was eaten, Matthew asked if he could say grace—and that he did, with amends echoing throughout the fine palace. This was a splendid meal, with warm stoned-baked bread and lamb stew made with the finest of vegetables. Cheeses and fruit were served to toast the end the hearty meal.

With great honor, Matthew and Althea enjoyed their first feast in the castle. Here, they had announced their engagement—their pledge to all eternity. Althea felt the silver ring on her left hand, with the heart facing her. She had been taken, and her prince would always lead her way.

As they enjoyed the meal, Mrs. McCormick seemed in a distant daze. She had dreamed of this moment only earlier in the month, all before she had any idea that Matthew and his beloved had arrived. She was also overcome with the sighting of the claddagh on the Glory Stones at the Great Falls. She had been told by her ancestors that the pond had once been enchanted by a goddess and her long-lost love from another world. She had laughed at the legend, but here was the miracle that made the legend unique and accountable.

Mr. McCormick was concerned about his proud wife; she seemed distant. He filled her mug to the brim and kissed her ruddy cheeks. She looked into his eyes with love and admiration. She suddenly felt giddy and freshly "in love" with her dear old hubby of thirty years. This would be a day and night they would always remember. Little Sean was a late arrival in their family and was excited and completely enamored of the new lady of the house. He danced about and sang his Irish tunes, for Sean was a musical lad who could sing like an angel. All was good in this warm Irish kitchen, with a family lovingly assembled and thinking about a bright and hopeful tomorrow.

The pleasurable evening darkened to the sacred night. Matthew toured Althea through the castle. She was astounded by the magnificence of the dwelling. Although large, the furnishings and carpets gave it a familiar coziness. The elegant drapery provided intimacy and warmth to the stone walls. Lush carpets with tassels and elaborate designs softened the feel of the hard stone floor. The furnishings were sparse but stately and comfortable.

Matthew escorted Althea to the upper quarters. Matthew stroked Althea's back and pointed to a special area in the castle. "Yes?" said Althea. "Is this something of interest?" Matthew delightfully stated, "This room will be your favorite, my heirloom lassie." He wanted to show her a room that would warm and delight her—the children's nursery. Many a child had been placed here in the safety of the fortress. Althea wandered around the precious room and touched the wooden cradle, which began to rock gently to and fro. At that moment, something else began to rock to and fro, deep within her body, and it was then, that she was certain that she was rich with child, and yet ...

As Matthew gently took Althea's arm, he noticed that she was overcome with emotion and fatigue. He had forgotten how much she had experienced. Indeed, she felt extremely fatigued, and Matthew took her to the suite that they would share—she had her quarters, and he had his, but they were joined by a private door for their privacy and happiness.

Despite her exhaustion, Althea looked deeply into Matthew's gentle eyes and stated slowly and seductively, "This is my favorite room, my love, as it is the beginning of a busy nursery." Grinning yet surprised, Matthew again saw the exhaustion in her face as he took her to the old wooden four-poster bed. He ordered her to rest and said that Mrs. McCormick would attend to her needs. She looked into his eyes and said, "Aye, my captain, I do as you order." Althea used a dark and masculine voice, and Matthew smiled in glee and thought how wonderfully captivating and alluring his Althea could be. She was the woman in his life and would forever be so.

Althea then became unusually quiet, and Matthew sensed her need for rest and privacy. He kissed her sweetly on her plump, pink lips and quietly left her to rest, saying, "Dreams of gold, my love." And with that, Althea dropped her exhausted frame gently upon the beautiful bed and immediately fell into a peaceful slumber.

Shortly, Mrs. McCormick came quietly into the room and lighted the grand fireplace that was shared in this dual master suite. She saw Althea resting, awakened her quietly, and then assisted her into a long white gown made with delicate lace. Althea complied but seemed lost in a dream. Mrs. McCormick knew of the love Althea and Matthew shared, because she had secretly witnessed the vision at the waterfall. She knew the young lassie was with child, and it was her duty to make sure that she and this child would forever remain safe and cared for.

Several hours later, in the still of the beginning of a long dark night, Althea awoke with a start; she could not remember where she was.

She looked into the next room and saw a fire burning dimly in the fireplace. The room was lighted by its flame, dimly but enough to see around. Althea rose and moved about the stately room. She carried a candle burning brightly, "Mrs., McCormick must have left it by her bedside." Althea thought fondly.

On a nearby wooden vanity was a pitcher of water, and she poured the mineral water into a pewter mug. As she sipped the cool water, she was quickly reminded of the moments when she and Matthew were submerged in the spring water. She drank deeply and slowly, filling her warmed body with the water that inspired life.

She picked up the silver hairbrush and began to brush her long hair. As she did, she gazed into a very special glass that reflected her feminine form. She was astounded to see herself, looking like a ghost in this beautiful long white gown with the delicate lacing.

Althea then found an armoire on the other side of the room, filled with dresses, capes, shoes, and other items that a lady could use. She was delighted but restrained herself from using anything until she spoke with Matthew.

She looked into the suite of the other room, stepping lightly, carrying the bedside candle, she walked into the grand room. Here she found no one, but many handsome leather-bound books awaited her attention. Althea had a passion for reading, so she carefully chose one. Her feet were cold, and the empty, warm bed looked inviting. She placed the burning candle on the bedside table and jumped into the draped master bed. She read by the light of the candle and the dim fire, with the full moon beaming through the bedroom window.

She had no idea of the time, but she did not care. She wondered where Matthew had gone, but she was not overly concerned.

She snuggled deeply into the fluffy, down bed and continued to read. After a short time, her strained eyes felt heavy, and at last, she surrendered to the drift of dreams taking her far away. ...

***

This was a place where seasons changed to cold temperatures, with freezing, biting rain that chilled a body to the bones in a matter of minutes. This was a season when extra bricks of peat moss would await their call of duty, a season to eat hearty foods and drink strong hot teas.

Althea was walking in an unusual ice-crystal, dark, world without sound. She was dressed in her long white gown, and her bare feet were chilled to the bone. The cold had consumed her, yet she was coherent and without a doubt knew, she was in a dream world.

This was a world with no sunshine or living creatures; there was only a silent, icy world, where life and death were one. Althea was frightened and began to call Matthew's name. "Matthew, where are you, my love? Please answer me." She sensed his presence, yet she could not find him. She wandered about, unable to see, and found nothing but ice-cold, black crystals of doom, frozen particles of dust, centuries old. She could not see and yet she knew the crystals were black, frozen bits of rough substance.

Suddenly, she bumped into a very hard object. Althea cried out in pain, "Oh, my heavenly Father, what is this, and where am I?" She reached through the icy mist and again called to Matthew, "Please, my love, answer me!" She reached down to find the obstacle that blocked her. Her hands studied the object, frozen and unmovable. After several moments, she realized it was a bed—a small cot—and she had bumped into the wooden leg. She immediately moved her fingers frantically to the top of the cot. When she touched the cold object, her delicate legs buckled. She dropped to her knees. Before her was a frozen body, and the flash of memory told her it was someone she knew—her love, her life, her future!

All through her chilled body, she felt the pang of fear and death. With control and desperation she bowed before him, praying that he was alive.

She had found him, and this had occurred in a frozen world of hell, a world where all crystals were frozen, black and light did not exist.

With trembling fingers, she touched the frozen body, feeling gently at first and then with a hurried, frantic search. As her fingers roamed the body, they came upon the frozen face. A great wall of pain shot through her chilled body. She screamed, but no sound came from her mouth. She convulsed, but her body remained still. She could not breathe, yet she was aware. Her body knew his body, now devoid of life. She could not fathom the idea of Matthew's frozen body upon this cot in the dark, ice-crystal world. She collapsed upon the frozen stone floor, with one hand remaining on his chest. At once, she felt warmth and a soft voice telling her to wake up.

Slowly, she opened her frightened eyes and cried, telling him of her dream. Matthew reassured her, "Althea, I am here. I am alive, as alive as any man could ever be." She was very cold—icy cold. Matthew brought her hot tea, and she sipped it quietly. Althea did not completely waken but fell back into a restless slumber.

***

Early the next morning, Althea opened her eyes, and sat up to look upon a quiet room, still glowing with a warm fire. Mrs. McCormick came to her and covered her shoulders with a warm shawl. Althea's body was damp with sweat, yet she was icy cold. There was fear in her face, and she would not speak. Eliza had been there during the nightmare and had given her an herbal tea that helped to settle the nerves and bring about a peaceful sleep.

Because of Althea's despondency, Eliza did not press her to speak. She knew at once the dream was from another world. This type of dream was a warning...possibly of a future event. With apprehension, Eliza understood such a dream would need to be exercised with caution and attentiveness.

All old Irish women knew that spirits and possessions sometimes occurred during a tragedy. These spirits were neither wicked nor saintly but a type of messenger, brought to warn or assist.

Again, Althea sipped the fragrant black tea, and then she began to drink it down rapidly as she tasted the sweetness. She was frightened and cold, but hungry. Eliza noticed this, and at once brought her warm bread, dipped in fresh butter. Althea gobbled it greedily and then finished the tea. Eliza was puzzled but smiled warmly at the beauty in the master's bed.

Althea had a flare for life and was visionary. Matthew had told Eliza of the tragedy she had experienced in her

French village close to the sea. Eliza was horrified that something so terrible could have happened—to witness the devastation would have been even worse. Althea refused to speak, she sat up higher in the bed, and at once became aware of the nightmare that had frenzied her mind and body.

She knew that Matthew was gone, and gone he would remain. Her sorrow was overwhelming. How could she endure more loss? Althea wanted to fall away into another world, but at that moment, she felt a gentle flutter in her body. In a silent state, she rose, and walked to the window and looked out of the window at the grand Atlantic Ocean. The day was misty and cool. Althea's heart was broken and nothing would change her feeling.

Eliza watched Althea and guided her back to her warm bed. Althea closed her eyes and fell into a gentle slumber. Reassured that Althea was alright, she left her to rest. She had chores to do and would return shortly. She placed the tray with the tea on the small table near the bed. As she stroked Althea's soft head, she noticed that she was clutching the tartan plaid of the MacDonnell clan. She clutched it to her heart and grasped it tightly. It was Matthew's, and somehow she had found it, or perhaps it had found her...

Her grip was strangely unique. The fine Scottish wool was well worn and slightly tattered. Althea had wrapped it around her body; such as the Scottish man would have done, before a traditional ceremony.

Eliza questioned Althea's gloom, thinking, "Why was she so distraught?" At that moment, Althea called out Matthew's name but began to speak in French, a language Eliza knew but not proficiently. Eliza did understand the gestures and composure on Althea's face. She looked like death; even the room seemed colder, and the day became darker.

Without another thought, Eliza refueled the fireplace, as even her own body began to feel the terrible cold circulating throughout the room. As the fire began to blaze, Althea seemed to calm and gaze into the fire. Again, in pure French, she shouted, "Death is not the end. Our love forever lives! Love will never leave us because our love is an eternal love!"

Eliza was frightened about the verse, and was able to translate it but not completely. She was concerned about the dear child, so consumed with death. Why in heaven's name had the sky darkened, and the room cooled? This was midday, the warmest time of the day. Eliza decided to remain with Althea, watching over her like a good nursemaid, a mother, a friend, Slowly, she sat down on a chair close to Althea, and with all the love and devotion of a priest, Eliza began to recite a comforting prayer that she had learned from her great-grandmother.

Within minutes, the sun began to beam its warm light through the window, and the fire began to blaze. Althea slumbered quietly, facing the blazing fireplace and slowly opened her somber eyes. Eliza had closed her eyes, rested her head against the cool stone wall, and fell into a deep sleep.

Althea did not notice the woman or the warm sunshine streaming into the room. Her eyes were fixated on the blue part of the flame. She clutched the soft tartan that smelled of Matthew. She glazed into the blue flame that began to roll like the waves of the Atlantic, the water moving with a powerful force, she heard the great roar of the water, as it crashed upon itself. She could smell the ocean—clean, fresh, and wild—and the grand room became the deck of the *Scottish Queen*.

Chapter 5: Matthew Leaves Ireland

*M*atthew knew that leaving Althea would be difficult. She had fallen asleep, but she needed some time to rest and build up her strength from her sorrows and the long voyage to Ireland. He would return quickly, giving her time to rest and settle herself into Delany Castle. The route to Scotland was short. He would take care of his military obligations and inform his family of his plan to marry Althea and live in the Irish castle. As he quickly left the Irish harbor, he recognized the tempest again awaiting his departure. He was determined and had seen similar skies, dark and ominous.

And indeed, another storm came to them, but Matthew and his crew fought the storm and, with determination, ended the journey safely at the Scottish coast.

After docking the *Scottish Queen*, he went below to grab his other

Military maps commanded by his Scottish commanders; they would remain with him. Their value was important to all naval captains, as the charting of the seas had yet to be done, and Matthew's voyages and maps would contribute a great knowledge to all.

As he returned to the deck, Matthew examined his vessel from bow to stern. The sails and mast had been damaged by the gusts of the violent storm. The long jib had been severely cracked; the stern had been severed and had taken in water. With a sigh, he knew the damage would detain him for some time, but he could send a message of his delay to someone going to Ireland.

In a flash, as Matthew descended the steps to his captain's quarters, he saw a woman dressed in white... trying to hide herself. He rubbed his tired eyes. He had not slept and was extremely fatigued. He was certain he had seen a ghost. The apparition had resembled Althea—long honey-blonde hair and the strong feminine body. Matthew was not certain of his mental state and dismissed the thought of seeing anything, thinking he was a lad in love, thinking about his lady.

As he entered the captain's quarters, he smelled her fragrant skin and heard the rustling of someone moving. He looked around frantically, and still finding nothing.

At once, feeling overwhelmingly warm and drawn to his bed, the lair of he and his love, he craved to lie with her and sleep. He could feel her loving embrace and her quiet sounds. Matthew shook himself and splashed his face with water from the bucket next to his bed. He tried to ignore this strange instinct to remain and sleep—he desperately needed the rest, and he felt a strange longing to just lie down and sleep, and dream of his beautiful lady.

In a snap, he broke himself of this alluring spell and proceeded in his endeavor to complete his plan. As he reached to retrieve the navigation maps below the dressing table, he spotted Althea's cameo charm necklace, the one she had worn on her neck. Its beauty reminded him of the love they shared, and without another thought, he lifted the cameo and placed it in his palm. He instantly felt the warmth and tenderness of her love, beckoning him to stop and sleep. But his duty was at hand, so he carefully placed the cameo deeply in the pocket of his sailor trousers, "The heavens rolled dark clouds and children rose in their warm nests far away..."

Quickly, he returned to the deck and spoke with his crew; they were fatigued and depressed. One had actually been lost at sea. They felt an omen, and their only plight was to remain onboard. They were a tight-knit crew, and this loss had them searching their souls. Matthew told them to stay aboard until he returned. He would make arrangements to have the broken ship restored to its working condition. The crew felt heavy and forlorn...warning Matthew. He had felt the heavy toll of leaving Althea, for he had left her without her knowledge; of course, the McCormick's would explain the reason for his quick departure. He was discouraged and worried. And now to watch his crew...sad and angered by his departure. With determination, he toiled. He must not fret; time moved forward.

Matthew carried the cameo in his pocket, making an oath to ask Althea to forgive him for leaving her unannounced. With wonderment, he and his crew had found many abandoned boats floating in the quiet harbor. The crew had been puzzled, and Matthew demanded their immediate attention to anchor the floating vessel. Matthew called out, "I shall return shortly, rest my good men."

With courage and fortitude, Matthew rushed to the village and found it vacant and quiet; he was relieved, after seeing the burned and looted French village, he had expected to see the worst. The seemingly abandoned village was intact with no apparent looting or fires.

He rushed to his home and rapidly approached the gateway to his family estate; he noticed that it had not been broken or vandalized. Immediately, he spied one of the workers that assisted his mother with the garden and the labor around the estate. Matthew was again encouraged and made his presence be known. The old man was sitting on the rock step of the deserted home; he had been with the family most of his life. Matthew gently greeted him. "MacGregor, it is I, Matthew. Are you well, sir? Where is my family?"

The old fellow was distant and seemed incoherent. The air was silent, but a gentle ocean breeze seemed to break the quiet tension. Matthew spoke again, louder and bolder, "MacGregor! In God's name, what has happened? Speak to me, now! I demand you, old man." Matthew sat next to him for a moment, unsure of what to do. After several long minutes, Matthew shook his head, nervous and anxious to find his family. MacGregor appeared lost in a dream, unable to rouse himself. He left the old man sitting on the step of his childhood home.

Matthew then entered the two-story stone home, inhaling the fragrance of home, yet feeling the sadness of its vacancy, he called out in a weary voice, "Mama, are you here? Anyone? Come out at once! It is I, Matthew MacDonnell." No reply echoed to him, only silence, and a sad and lonely silence. As he exited his home, Matthew again saw an apparition, the same one he saw in the ship, "She was angelic and said to him, "Leave at once my love, return to me, return to your family."

Feeling strangely alone and unaware of the reasons the house had been abandoned—his childhood dwelling—Matthew walked slowly through the old home and then left with a bewildered expression. He was feeling lost and uncertain.

He stepped down the stone steps and approached old MacGregor with sadness in his eyes and a feeling of quiet desperation. The old man looked deeply into Matthew's eyes and surprisingly stated, "My lad, you are late. Your family is gone. Your father is imprisoned and is long gone."

Matthew gave MacGregor a gentle embrace and, realizing he needed assistance, carefully guided him into the old stone home. "MacGregor, stay here and rest your weary mind and body. I will return shortly to assist you and the others to safety. Where are they, MacGregor?"

MacGregor looked up and mumbled a weak answer... "Go to the old McKenzie castle. It is there he has been incarcerated. Go at once, boy. Time is not on your side."

With that Matthew, turned and left the old man and the deserted family home.

He rushed to the old castle. It had once belonged to the Mackenzie's, but that was many years ago. The castle had been converted and was now used as a town common property, where the government was headquartered, all within a quick walk of the stone fortress of his home. The MacDonnell family had frequently visited, and Matthew knew the shortest route.

Matthew moved along the narrow cobblestone road that twisted through the quaint Scottish village. As he walked, he was reminded of his life here and felt warm, but strangely torn. He had always been so compliant of his parents' demands. He remembered his desire to be a rebellious youth, trying to control his own destiny, live his life as he pleased, despite the fact that his family had made decisions to take complete control of his future.

He rushed to the old government structure that hailed its power through solid walls of stone. Matthew heard the sounds of revolt and anger drifting through the entrance. The dialect was that of the English soldiers; Matthew had encountered many, in the English harbors where he had anchored his ship. Overhearing the thunderous sounds of the English soldiers, Matthew cringed, "Now we are to take control of the upper county, and that we shall do!"

As Matthew heard the declarations, he was at once defensive of the sounds of the brutal demands of entitlement. As he entered the building, he was grabbed by a soldier for no reason, other than his presence. Upon the assault, Matthew fought back, and at once several large guards grabbed him and demanded to see his papers. "We are to know at once who you are and what business you have."

Matthew was angered by their brutal demands and did not submit his papers or his status. He demanded information of his lost family and on what order the English had infiltrated this peaceful village. Matthew's attitude did not appease the guards; in fact, they became even more hostile and angry.

Twisting Matthew's arms in a menacing gesture, they demanded obedience. Matthew fought them with fevered passion and at once, they became even more violent and demanding. Matthew was brutally cuffed, tied, and thrown into a small cell close to the entryway. With retaliatory behavior, Matthew managed to break loose and throw a fierce punch into the gut of one of his captors. Grunting loudly, the guards began to viciously beat Matthew, with forceful slugs landing on his face, bringing blood quickly to the surface and spilling down his weary face. There was another punch, followed by an even harder blow to his abdominal area and rib cage. The blow to the rib cage was enough to force Matthew to the hard, stone floor. He had lost consciousness in the middle of this torturous beating, and so the guards left him, bloody and quiet.

When Matthew began to regain his consciousness he heard them return. The merciless guards snarled at Matthew, "Tell us now why your father will not sign the oath of alliance."

Matthew did not reply. In a desperate attempt to force his escape, he began to fight them again, kicking his assailants with every bit of his might and courage that flowed through the blood of an old Viking warrior. The wicked soldiers laughed and finally held him down. An old English guard approached him with caution and exclaimed, "I see you have not the intelligence or the dignity to surrender your pathetic presence to the new rule of the land."

Matthew surrendered. "I beg of you to allow me to present my navigation maps to your captain. They are invaluable. I have been at sea, taking great care to record my travels."

The ignorant, wicked guards bellowed their obnoxious laughter and kicked Matthew's tortured head, now bloodied and with a mouth of missing teeth and a mind unconscious to the malicious beatings inflicted upon his bloody and broken body.

Later that evening, Matthew came to his senses and realized he had been imprisoned—he had been dragged into a cold, dark cell. The smell of mold and urine wafted through his lungs, creating a nauseating urge to release the vials of his sufferings, to vomit profusely.

He was devastated and lost in bewilderment, but he was coherent, and with a determined spirit, he thought, *I have not been home for more than a year. Surely the city has not been taken over by violent protestors. Could this violent war be upon my native land, so far away from the rest of Europe?* He called often to his captors, and when they returned, they asked him for his papers. Matthew declared boldly, "Aye, I am a Scottish citizen and sworn military officer."

The war-torn and dirty faces of the guards seemed unaffected, and with a thick English accent, they hollered. "Ah, and what good does that do ye now?" They laughed at him and informed him of his status. "You are a threat to Prince William and Lady Mary, and we are here to see that you no longer proceed. You now have no power here, until we have the signature so demanded by our king!"

Matthew pleaded to them, "You bloody brutes, I am a navigator of the dark oceans. I have found many great passages that will help your king to lead his military ships and expeditions. I beg of you to release me, so that I may share this great knowledge with you and that of your great king." Matthew also informed them that he had been away for more than a year and had no ties to his city or government, except his duties to navigate the dark waters of the sea. "I apologize for my haste, but I go in peace, and I declare my knowledge to one and all." Matthew stated his full name and residence. He was hoping that his family status would clarify his good motives.

Instead, his captors looked even more angry and hostile. One of the brutes stated with cynicism, "Ah your father is an important man here—so important that he now lives in the dungeon of this old fortress."

Matthew pressed on. "What have you done with my father? Incarcerated? Here? He would not harm the king, nor would his actions."

They replied in their hostile, ignorant brogue, "We need his bloody signature, and the rotten bloke won't sign the covenant. Bloody hell with 'im! Let the bastard die! Off with 'is bloody head! Let 'im rot in this place!"

Matthew became silent in thought. *Yes, indeed that would be the way of an old warrior; he would give his life for his convictions.* Matthew felt the terror of concern for his father and the location and safety of his family. He was determined to make right of the situation and respectfully said, "I beg you to take me to see my father. Perhaps I can help him to understand your demands." The guards scolded him and told him to be still. Out of fear and terror, Matthew silenced himself, wanting to give his thoughts to his father.

Later, the guards brought him water in an old tin pitcher and a loaf of dried bread. Matthew was determined to find his father and make a plan of escape. Again, he made an attempt to convince the guards of his innocence but to no avail. The guards responded with nothing more than grunts and snickers.

After drinking the water and eating the hard bread, he felt the pain of the confrontation and the fatigue of the journey. Matthew willed himself to rest and finally to sleep. He had found an old cot made of straw and grasses. He dozed with thoughts of Althea and his lost family. Where had they gone? Were they in danger? His thoughts displayed the horror of the French village, massacred beyond his worst nightmare. The bodies strewn about, bloodied and burned.

In heaven's name, he could never fathom the death and destruction of his own family—any family—as Althea's family was as near to him as his own. The horror of this discovery had scalded Matthew's mind and left him wondering as to the reality of a world gone astray. Dry tears fell from his wounded heart. He alone could make a difference in the lives of so many, yet he was anchored in this hellhole, surrounded by beasts with the mind of a puppet, used by a king with unscrupulous morals and the dignity of a half-wit. Matthew's heart and mind became intertwined in defeat. The stench of the dark, dank prison had begun to depress his ambition, but he was determined to move forward.

His broken body, his aching limbs, and his skull bloodied and beaten, bashed to bits had begun to throb with every beat of his heart. He was covered with dried blood, and his clothing smelled of his own excrement. He could hear the rustle of varmints and the flutter of the bats that resided here.

In desperation, he reached out to grasp for God, and then he dug his nails into the soft dark stone surrounding his existence. Finally, in a clouded consciousness, he awoke in a blaze of fever, his body covered with a sweat, yet he felt chilled to the bone. His loneliness and fears brought him farther into the depths of his own sanity.

Matthew lay there, repenting his sins, begging God to forgive him so he could escape, help his family, and return to Althea. He heard the sounds of the distant guards as they plodded across the hard stone floor. "Is the traitor dead yet?" they bellowed. "What are we to do with him? He is the son of the other stubborn fool who called himself the warrior. We will keep them incarcerated, as that is their choice, and then we shall be rewarded for our bravery. These people are to be extinguished—all they are and all they believe in."

Later, the angry guards entered the dark cell and dragged Matthew's injured body to an area deep within the old castle, an area darker and colder. The moisture in the air floated like a dark icy cloud, and the visibility was as dark as the midnight sky. Again, the sound of scampering rodents filled Matthew with the dread of disease. These areas were sometimes used for the prisoners and those dying of questionable diseases, a horrible and bleak place to be or die.

Matthew was miserable and fought the guards upon their return to his cell. His act of defiance only angered the guards, and again they attacked him, ruthlessly and without restraint. They tossed his limp body, and as he was dumped onto the frozen dungeon floor.

Matthew became aware of his own smell of death and the pungent odor of rotting flesh.

The freezing temperatures of the icy dungeon had preserved the worst part of death's shadow. Matthew begged the guards to listen to him and help him return to his family. He pleaded to them and even bribed them, asking them to allow him to leave this dark world. They did listen but gave no indication to help. They sent bread and water on a tray. In anger and defeat, Matthew threw it to the floor and adamantly demanded to see his father.

They laughed and shoved a large parchment paper into his bloodied face. "Find your father and tell him to sign the covenant, and you shall both go free." As they left, Matthew heard them laughing like the devil after a destructive match with the innocent. Like a gallant warrior, Matthew shouted at them with ancient words from his native tongue. He sounded the words with all the strength and passion left in his tortured body. Afterward, Matthew only heard the waning sounds of laughter and lewd comments.

After a many dark and sad hours, Matthew began to sense that he was in the presence of another person. He could not see or hear anyone, but somehow he felt a nearness of someone, somewhere. Immediately, his thoughts and hopes to see his father helped him regain strength. *I must find a way to clear my head and try to find my father. He will know what to do, how to appease the guards, and possibly fulfill their demands.* He would convince his stubborn father to comply with their requests or do whatever would be necessary to escape this wicked entrapment.

After what seemed like an hours, Matthew realized he was dreaming. Matthew knew that he must try to survive, and despite his injured and bloodied body, he managed to find the bread left earlier by the guards. He did his best to gnaw on the hard, coarse food, even though he could feel his gums tearing and bleeding. He reached out for the water, but the jug of water had spilled.

Like a gleam of hope, Matthew heard the faint sound of dripping water, possibly an old dripping faucet, near the back of the chamber. He heard the incessant sound of water hitting the surface with a *zink-zink, zink-zink.* The sound had relaxed him and now, with the knowledge of its origin and its wonder, Matthew forced himself to find it and partake of its blessing—and perhaps find a way to trace the outlet for an escape to his freedom. Matthew approached the water, dripping with a reverent purpose. He placed his shaking hands in the water and formed a cup, and from this cup he swallowed the liquid, and then he splashed his bloodied skin, washing some of the debris that had adhered to his face.

It was at this magical moment that he recalled the afternoon he and Althea were bathing in the mineral spring near his Irish castle. Their love was united, and the Gods had blessed them and filled their bodies with a union of Scottish-Viking blood, mixed with that of the French blood of royalty crowned with the sacred thorns. This memory, like a ray of sunshine, filled his heart with love. He drank of this water and rejoiced in the fact he had found the memories of everlasting life. Matthew's mind began to venture to his past life and how he had been given life through love, enduring all time and obstacles.

After several hours of restless sleep, Matthew awakened. He realized his violent outburst with the guards was something he would regret. He rarely lost his temper, but this incident brought out his weaknesses. And his weaknesses would overrule his ability to rise from this treacherous incarceration. He begged for another opportunity to confront the guards, amicably and in control.

The darkness of the dungeon left him almost unable to see, but now his eyes had begun to adjust to the darkness, and with determination he moved about, trying to locate his father. This room was not a cell but a large chamber, with many other rooms, each darker than the one he had entered. He realized he was deep within the bowels of the old castle. It was dark, cold, and very damp. His eyes were badly swollen, and one of his ribs must have been broken, because the pain was excruciating. Matthew tried calling to his father—or to anyone who might answer—but to no avail. He was abandoned in this place, and he would have to find an escape. Frantically, he crawled through the darkest of the chambers, using his injured and bloodied fingers to search for the remains of a body. He was aware of the odor of a dead body, possibly his father. He bowed his head in fear and distress. Matthew felt the surge of grief rise throughout his beaten body, ready to mold itself to a cross of hope. He would find his father and together, they would reunite through their determination to escape this treachery. Matthew was determined to find his father, regardless of his condition. The coldness of the dungeon must have limited the odor of death and yet the odor of death penetrated his mind.

Matthew crawled and moved on hands and knees, his eyes almost swollen shut, and yet somehow he could see through the dark, as if he were guided by a mysterious compass...

After several days or hours, Matthew was uncertain of time, he heard a faint stirring, a rustling, and then a weak muttering, a prayer, a song. Following the sound and with a small spark of hope Matthew moved quickly, without experiencing the pain and fatigue, and at last...a body, the body of his father. In disbelief and joy, Matthew wept, and put his head to his father's chest. "Was this man alive?" Matthew thought to himself. The body cold, and deadly still, yet he had heard the sounds...

As Matthew rested his head he thought, "Here was his honored and self-made royal father, dead in the bowels of this old fortress. Matthew wept and refused to believe that he, too, would die this way!"

Within moments Matthew heard the feeble voice of his father, "Matthew, my son ... is that you?"

Matthew looked up. He was startled; his father's body had been deathly cold. *How can this be?* Matthew immediately answered, "Father, is that you? It is I, your son, Matthew." Matthew reached out to him and held him like a child. Tears fell from his bloodied and bruised eyes. He felt the rhythm of his father's strong heart and felt the peace a son receives from a good father.

Matthew's memories rekindled to those of days gone by—days when he was a boy, with a family that knew love and the endearing, strong family bond. Matthew gently spoke to his dear father. "Father, what has happened? Where are mother and the family?"

Sadly, his father replied, "Your family is in exile from this war-torn land. They have sailed to England to be near your mother's family. You must go to them, Matthew."

Matthew reassured the old, dying warrior, "Father, I will go at once, but what has happened to you?"

His father answered, "I am a dying man, and I have served my purpose. Leave me at once and assist them, rescue your kin...let me be!"

"My honorable father, I beg you—tell me of your incarceration. Why have they done this to you?"

"Ah, lad, you must know our land has been captured by the evils of a reformation that curdles the blood of all our people."

Matthew remained silent for a few moments. He then asked, "Why did you not sign the covenant? It is only a document, a parcel filed in the king's office. It means nothing!"

"Ah, but I am an old warrior, with blood that binds the heart with the signature. If I were to sign that covenant, I would give away my word and the work of all my ancestors."

Matthew knew his father would never change. No longer would he bother his father to conform, even if it meant freedom from this prison.

Matthew wanted to help his dying parent, so he stumbled to the water dripping gently in the back of the dark and dank prison cell. He clasped his palms together, and collected the dripping water and brought it to this old warrior, his father, his mentor, his friend.

As his father and he sipped the water, Matthew noticed it tasted strangely sweet and seemed familiar. "You are a good son, Matthew, and I have always been proud of you, but I have missed you. I am glad you have returned." His father was comforted and relieved by Matthew's care and patience.

Matthew remembered the fragments of dried bread he had placed in the pocket of his pants. He broke a small piece of the bread that at once became fresh and sweet. He crumbled a small piece and lifted his father's head, so that he could partake of this sacred meal. Matthew knew that the strange magic was the blessings of the warrior blood that surrounded all dying warriors.

His father's face took on some color, and his dark blue eyes lit up with warmth. "My good son, I am forever indebted and honored that you are to be with me at these last moments. You carry our future. I see your unborn children in your eyes."

Matthew was surprised, "How could his father say such stories?" At once Matthew remembered his Althea. With his dying father in his arms, he began to tell his story of the love that had entered his life. With great care, he spoke gently and sincerely. "Father, I have found my love, the love that gives me purpose, the love that makes me whole. We

73

are to be wed as soon as I can return to her. She carries our babes!"

The old warrior sighed and hesitated but immediately opened his blue eyes that twinkled with victory. "And my son... sighed the old warrior "Why in God's name are you here with me?

Matthew was perplexed and taken aback. Sensing his trouble the old warrior called out with a bold voice.

"We have won the battle, and now, my great son, go to war! We shall reign victoriously. No dungeon will defeat our purpose. Your babes carry the blood of our forefathers."

Matthew asked gently, "Bless our union, Father? We shall be married in the church!" With the proud voice of a wise and stately man he replied, "Son, you are already blessed, the life is your blessing, you do not need me. I treasure your request, but it is unnecessary. Love is the blessing in itself. But as a soldier and a father of tradition, I will do as you wish."

With a grand strength and a final announcement, he proclaimed to Matthew and to the world, "I have blessed you and the lady of your world and also those eternally on this almighty earth. May you live in harmony with a bountiful life!"

Matthew was filled with relief and joy, as his father had been adamant about the previous marriage promise, yet he now seemed forgiving and passionate about this blessing. Matthew dropped his head upon his father's chest and clutched him as a loving son. "Father, I love you, and I will remember our bond. That bond will live within my heart and the hearts of my heirs." Matthew heard his father gasp a long, deep breath and murmur a quiet prayer. He had heard his father speak in a Slavic language, reserved for times when no other words were applicable. Those strong words were his last. And with that, the old man became limp and silent in the arms of his precious son. The life of an ancient and gallant warrior retired itself within the bowels of this old Scottish castle. Matthew mourned his death, yet hailed the dignity of a man so honorable and courageous.

Matthew slowly moved his weary body to the front entry of the dark room. With all his might, he shouted, "Guards! Guards! Come here at once. I demand of you and your king to come to me and assist me with the suffering of my father. His death looms. I shall not let him die in vain." Matthew waited and clung to the cold bars of the prison cell. The air was frozen around his face, and the spirit of death surrounded him. He waited, but no one came to his aid. Feeling strangely alone and yet hopeful, Matthew realized that he and his father had reconciled. Never before had they spoken so true and brave. All the harbored pain and guilt had been released; Matthew began to feel a type of peace and a new strength of acceptance. Matthew's father had forgiven him and given him and Althea his blessing of future happiness. More than ever, Matthew was determined to leave this chamber and return to Althea and their growing babes, but this time he would go with the promise of his father's dying blessing. Matthew knew in his weary heart that love would guide him, and he would forever be with his love.

Feeling the strange weakness in his legs and the slow, vacant beat of his heart, Matthew had become aware of an inevitable realization—his own mortality, his life force, was at stake. He knew that he must rest and plead to God for his strength and ability to escape this entrapment. His moved his weary body back to the old cot. He collapsed and made a promise to himself that he would escape this dungeon to carry out his father's demands. He would escape this treacherous situation and return to Althea and then journey on to England to retrieve his mother and sisters. All would be well; this incarceration would be short, and his life would move on. As Matthew's mind began to fill with the hope of his future, he realized that he was having difficulty and needed to rest. He was not sure of his own sanity. He needed to rest. The death of his father and the hope of returning to his family was overwhelming.

Sleeping for what could have been hours or even days, Matthew awakened shaking with cold and perspiration rolling down his forehead. He had been in a tortured dream, he was in a faraway world, a world foreign to him. Another world where the truth no longer mattered. A would that was ruled by the powerful and ambitious. And he was in the center right. This was a strange and sad feeling.

He began to feel a penetrating warmth. This heat radiated from the pocket of his trousers. He reached and slowly retrieved the delicate cameo. He then placed the comforting charm to his heart, and as he did, he discovered several strands of Althea's long hair tangled in the clasp. He cried tears of joy, realizing that a part of Althea was here. As he bowed his head to say his prayers, he heard her sweet voice calling to him. *"Matthew, I am here. Please take my warm hand. I will lead you out of this darkness to the light."*

Matthew reached out again, trying to clasp Althea's long, warm fingers. He reached for her, but not finding her hand, he desperately called to her, "My love, where are you? I cannot find you." Althea's voice did not reply, and as he desperately stretched his bloodied arm to her, he found only a cold wall covered with frozen, dark crystals...

As Matthew passed, he vowed to God that he would return to Althea, no matter how great the cost. His death would be avenged. He would someday, somehow, return to the world and tell them of his innocent incarceration and the death of his father, a great Viking warrior soldier, in this godforsaken dungeon. He would somehow join Althea and announce to the world of their sacred love, a love blessed from above. He remembered the shadows of the claddagh and the rainbows of light beaming on the woolen blankets, meant for his unborn children.

However great the cost, he would not be forsaken of the love he was destined to share with his lady, his princess, the mother of his children.

Chapter 6: Four Hundred Years Later in Riverbay Courthouse

*C*olette Peters was anxious, but relieved to be out of her busy classroom with the usual routine, molding the rebellious minds of eighth graders ready to conquer the world.

In this old, church parking lot she was desperately trying to find a place to park her well maintained compact Prious. This time she would find a place that was closer and more accessible to the courthouse. She had examined the jury summons map that displayed the parking lot locations and had made a plan, unlike her previous summons.

Collette anticipated the yearly jury calls and again wanted to see the judicial procedure in action. She parked her car under the tree of a California Oak. This lot was designated for the summoned jury. She felt secure knowing her car was here, in the shade, waiting for her return.

Even though she was nervous with anticipation, she looked professional and put-together. Her long blonde hair was styled in an elegant coif, drawn up on the back of her head and secured with a chic comb.

Feeling unsure of herself for some uncertain reason, perhaps because she was in a new place and surrounded by courthouses, police officers, prisoners; a world completely different than a middle school...

She laughed at herself and her rascals, realizing that the substitute would have them begging for her return. Despite her anticipation of the upcoming protocol, she had a smile on her face and a classy style in her walk. "If only she didn't stumble, or drop her handbag, she thought broodingly. On this early spring morning, the warm California sunshine beamed through a clear blue sky. She felt at ease with the world—except for her rocky marriage.

Every year, she contemplated filing for a divorce, but her daughter and career took priority. She thought Eliot would change, that his brutal put-downs and weeklong mysterious disappearances would stop. She had done everything to keep up her duties as a wife. She had lost her "mommy weight" and had shaped up by jogging and lifting weights at the local fitness club—she was there at least five days a week. In fact, she had brought her workout clothes with her, so she could put in a few hours after her work here.

Even though she wanted to find herself on the jury, she really doubted if she would be chosen. She was nervous and quite uncertain about crime and civil procedures.

She dismissed the thoughts of her husband. He did have a good side, the side she loved and cherished. After all, he had given her the greatest treasure: Sofia, her beautiful, intelligent daughter. Sofia was tall and sweet, with a brain that absorbed like a sponge. She had been reading since the age of four; Collette had been reading to her before she was born.

As she waited patiently for the red trolley that transported people within the city and jurors for free, she was startled by the sound of police sirens rapidly approaching. First, a small white compact car went flying by, and in pursuit were the two black-and-whites, almost on the tailpipe of the fleeting vehicle. They were moving at high speeds, way too fast for safety.

Collette and the group of people waiting for the trolley froze and watched the pursuit. Pursuits were not uncommon in California; in fact, the nightly news would often broadcast an exciting and frightening chase. Collette had watched several, sometimes lasting hours. She was remembering the case of the lost and out of control desperate man, allegedly killing his pregnant wife in a shower, and dumping her body in a lake. He had been caught, and had been on the run and was finally located by an exhausted officer, trying to maintain the peace. This man had been running from the police for hours on end, the media followed every move. Collette had been pregnant with her baby...she had watched the sad episode all day while preparing for her daughter's birth.

Hearing the siren's warning, she realized, all had been in danger of being injured by this out-of-control driver—the chase had been extremely close, just a couple of yards away, which put their own bodies in the path of danger. Collette tried to quiet the frightened congregation of people with her humor. She was aware of the danger of these pursuits, but she knew that the police had an important duty. Still, how many innocent bystanders would be victimized by a "chase gone bad" especially in a city street with many pedestrians?

The group of citizens quickly entered the trolley, wanting the feeling of security after observing the volatile scene. After taking a seat, Collette looked at the beauty of the landscaping. California was famous for roadsides that were always bright with the colors of different types of flowering bushes and trees, much as she had seen during her three years in Italy teaching English to Italians. In this bustling city, the landscaping was done with flair, and the historical section had many large trees that were lush, full of foliage, and provided shade and grace to this Southern California city.

Within minutes, they arrived at the splendid courthouse. It was made of white shale rock, with massive pillars and widely spaced steps, inviting all to seek the justice they had hoped to be given. As she exited the charming red trolley, she left a small tip for the driver; the woman had been polite and informative about the use of the trolley. Collette appreciated people who were willing to help citizens, as she always seemed to be perplexed in a new place.

In awe, Collette gazed at the massive courthouse. She had read about the architecture and remembered that it was built with a Roman influence, denoting its grandness, its power, and its wholesomeness. Many statues were mounted on the tops of its side structures, all symbols of divine justice. The architect had designed it to resemble important French buildings located in Paris. There had been rumors that this building contained special documents that were inserted into a northeastern cornerstone. It was laid with great fanfare by the Lodge of Masons in 1904. Even President Roosevelt had attended the celebration of its dedication.

Collette wondered what secret messages were contained in that cornerstone.

The splendor of the building fascinated Collette, and she let the pride of the city fill her with a new self-awareness. The oppression of a poor marriage had hindered her mind. Now, she was happy to have been chosen for this special opportunity. She would tell her students about the experience, omitting anything that might be confidential, of course.

The culture contained within the court area was interesting and lively—food carts selling beverages and snacks, people handing out petitions or religious flyers, others sitting outside, waiting for their trials. Some were lost in thought, smoking and looking hardened and disappointed. Guards seemed to be about, giving her a sense of peace and security. *Gosh*, she admitted to herself, *the California peace officers always look sharp*. They were fit and dressed officially in their well-pressed shirts and olive-green pants. She had considered dating an officer before her marriage but was frightened by the danger of losing someone she loved to the duties of honor. How brave and dedicated they all were—the officers and their families.

Collette joined the line assembling outside of the courthouse doors. Here, they waited in different lines; the attorneys had a special line so they could enter the courtroom rapidly as they ran from courtroom to courtroom. These people were impeccably dressed, for the most part. They wore suits and dressed in shoes of fine Italian leather. Each was well groomed, with fresh haircuts and manicures. Collette felt comfortable around them, as she always tried to present herself in a professional manner, at least at work. She knew that the style of clothing had an impact on those she encountered; today she was dressed in a work suit. This was a courthouse, and out of respect for the law and herself, she looked sharp and put together.

The summons protocol was quick and efficient. Of course, she had been early, as was her habit. Collette always allowed extra time for a traffic jam or making an unexpected stop—her favorite was the local coffee shop for a steaming hot tea, lightly sweetened and topped off with milk. She was a tea drinker and treasured her moments to warm herself with the soothing liquid.

After proceeding through a screened metal detector, with little hesitation she entered the building. It was busy but organized and smelled of a library—a favorite place where Collette enjoyed spending time. She was aware of the diversity lurking about. Other than attorneys and police officers, she saw citizens with tattoos and funky haircuts. She also saw persons dressed in jeans and slacks and sometimes T-shirts. Some were dressed similar to her. She felt comfortable with most, but sometimes was uncertain with persons brought in by the police—she felt sad for them, knowing that their lives had probably been difficult. As she seated herself in the assembly room meant for the jurors, she chatted briefly with the people next to her. She tried to read, but the commotion distracted her. Attendance was called, and when they called her name on the speaker, Collette automatically answered with a clear reply: "Present."

Rules and other protocol were announced to inform the potential jurors of their obligation. This was completed quickly, and Collette did not find it tedious nor boring. Many of the summoned jurors were dismissed and others were assigned to other courtrooms. Collette remained calm and began to read from her novel. Just as she was beginning to relax and enjoy the story, she was called to meet on the fourth floor. She had been selected along with ninety other individuals for another screening process. The ninety persons waited with anticipation in the hallway of the courtroom, some seated on benches, but most standing, visiting or just observing. Courtroom 42 was the designated courtroom. In only a few moments they were called to enter. Walking quickly, Collette reached into her handbag to grab her cell and turn off the power, an explicit rule ordered by the court. At the same moment, a gruff woman guard rudely asked, "Did you just turn on your cell?" Collette was taken aback by the nasty attitude, as she was actually turning off the device. This was her first encounter with hostility. *Why was she so rude and overbearing?* Collette thought but then dismissed it, out of respect for the court. This courtroom guard, the one in the small room, between the corridor and the courtroom, behind the double doors...was only doing her job. The guard must have noticed that Collette was late coming into the courtroom, she had taken a brief pit stop... ladies room. The grouchy guard probably needed another cup of coffee and was only asserting her power.

Feeling embarrassed and eager to escape this foul woman, Collette quickly turned, not taking time to bother with someone so foul. Collette felt positive and ready to participate in her civil responsibility. She was eager to participate in this endeavor, though few people wanted to do so. Why was she so different? Collette entered the spacious courtroom but felt self-conscious and put on the spot after the gruff woman barked at her. She now just wanted to sit and not be noticed. With a quick decision, she placed herself immediately to the middle right, next to the aisle. She was dressed in her brown plaid pant suit and a cream turtleneck, which was too warm for comfort, so she quickly took off the jacket and made herself comfortable. She was wearing her black boots with the two-inch heels, not because they looked tough or gave her height but because they were comfortable and kept her leg muscles warm. She was a runner and liked to keep herself fit and safe, "nothing like a pair of good boots."

After she settled down, she began to observe the environment. First and foremost, the seats were cushioned with cloth and reclined. Wow, just like the movie theatre. Nice to be treated so well, serving a civil responsibility.

There were approximately one hundred seats, divided into sections. The summoned jury could sit as they chose. The district attorney was to the right of the judge, and the defense attorneys and defendants to the left. Collette just wanted to be anonymous and watch the action. There were no windows in this room, which Collette found stifling, but that was probably for security reasons. The jury panel contained fifteen seats and was located to the right of the judge on a raised platform. They were able to scan the courtroom easily with a slight move of the head. They could also be easily observed from most of the other seats in the courtroom.

Collette had chosen a seat behind the defense attorneys, trying to be inconspicuous. She still felt embarrassed for being barked at by the rude guard, like getting slapped in the face for innocently doing the right thing. *Oh well,* she thought, *I can handle the grief.* She had become thick-skinned, yet still remained sensitive to the needs of others.

The case was cited, and Collette began to feel apprehensive. It was a case of a drug deal gone God Awful bad. No one was physically hurt, but children were involved and the drama sounded like a novel no one would want to read.

This was a world unknown to her, but at least it wasn't a murder trial, like the other one she had been paneled for. That one had her shaking and dreaming of nightmares for a week. Some gang dude had car jacked a vehicle and the other gang dude, messed up on some drug accidently shot and killed his partner in crime. The case was complicated and would certainly cost the taxpayers a briefcase or two of greenbacks.

Collette noticed that both defendants were represented by different attorneys. They seemed at home here in this courtroom, talking quietly and moving around with an ease Collette certainly did not have, at least here, in this courtroom.

As she gazed into the faces of the defendants, she felt a cold terror run down her spine. She had lived in a glass house and tried not to throw stones, always because someone else consistently did that. Her unhappy husband was always on a rant and took it upon himself to take a beg dump on her whenever he wanted. His stones only shattered her glass house. Here were large boulders that could destroy house in an instant.

One of the accused had a small black tattoo under his right eye. Collette had heard rumors or misconceptions about men sporting tattoos on their faces, especially men who had spent time in prison.

He was not a tall man and built with a stocky frame. He had long brown hair, gathered in a braid down his back. He was most definitely part Native American, perhaps full blooded Native American. His face seemed vacant and unnerving. Collette did not fear him though, he seemed to have the aura of an "eagle with clipped wings..."

She would not let this stop her from being fair and impartial. That was her duty, and she would do her best not to stereotype him, just because he had a tattoo under his eye. It resembled a teardrop or perhaps a heart. She was too far away to identify the symbol. But, she had heard several times that a man with a facial tattoo under an eye signified he had killed someone in prison...

The other defendant was older and had slicked-back gray hair. He had a hard expression on his face that seemed to show he had nerves of steel. His demeanor terrified her, and she thought it best not to look at him very long.

Collette guessed he was older than the other defendant by fifteen years or so. He looked angry, as if life had been tough for him, and he lived it as tough as it came to him.

She always felt sympathetic toward criminals and questioned why they had been accused of a crime. Whether they were guilty or innocent, Collette wondered what kind of life they had lived. They had all been someone's gift; mother, a father, a blessing from God.

The victims of crime were her main concern, but her empathetic side thought how all adults—criminals or priests—had once been children, born innocent and pure. What would entice them to commit such evil doings, if that is what they did? Collette did not express her fears; she would stay neutral, and she felt safe. After all, the alert guards were here and would take care of anything that might bring anyone harm. The police officers were alert and ready for confrontation, if necessary. She liked to look at them but tried not to for long. One wore a name badge with an Italian name, and he reminded her again of Italy and the compassionate nature of the people there.

Officer Muldado had sparkling, warm brown eyes, and a very stylish haircut. "Clean-cut, sharp, and empathetic, wow that was a nice package" thought Collette. Even his eyes had that conditioned response, they continuously scanned the room, but with genuine warmth. He had actually visited with the others in the courtroom with a friendly attitude, maintaining a guarded expression. Collette was impressed, "These people are top of the field. We are in good hands."

Collette checked the time. She felt a pang of sentimentality for her students, but was eager to complete her duties. She watched the judge closely, with great respect. She liked him immediately. He was quiet but jovial; he was tolerant but ran a tight ship. She liked his bow tie. It was a nice change that reminded Collette of the style of men in the East Coast. She loved New York City and had lived there off and on for many years.

This judge reminded her also of university professors from in her home state of Michigan. Judge Hobbs had kind eyes, but he was as observant as an old owl looking for its prey. He was balding but handsome and very well groomed. He and the attorneys and the police officers had a rapport that seemed casual and even sometimes with an air of humor. This was their workplace, and they apparently liked their duties.

This reminded Collette of her colleagues. They also laughed and joked around, but could be deadly serious and professional when they were working.

She again felt at ease and wanted to stay around. She realized the burden of a life decision she might have to make if she were chosen for the jury panel—a decision that would affect someone's life. She would remain committed to be fair and impartial.

The selection was lengthy but interesting. All the potential jurors were given a list of questions to answer to the judge and the attorneys—simple questions about themselves, their families, their occupations. Each person was to give a brief description of his or her life and then would be questioned by each attorney, who then would decide to dismiss or keep that juror. If the person was accepted by both counsels, the juror was then put on the panel.

Most of the ninety prospective jurors were adamant about *not* wanting to be selected; some were actually argumentative and annoyed. Most had some kind of excuse. This reminded Collette of her students and how they worked to find an excuse to get them out of completing their homework.

Judge Hobbs listened carefully to each of them and was tolerant but firm. Usually, they were dismissed. Collette was especially daunted by a man who had almost shouted at the court because he was so angry over being subjected to such an inconvenience as jury duty. He supported his beliefs well. Judge Hobbs quietly dismissed him and continued the selection process. Collette would mark that down on her list of behaviors to remember.

After a long day of listening to responses, the judge called it a day and dismissed the court, but he firmly instructed all to report the next morning, bright and early. Collette was thankful to leave the stuffy room. She had learned a great deal, but her patience was running thin. This process was time-consuming and tedious. She had planned to go to her fitness club and put in two hours, running and lifting weights, but instead, she felt the need to rest and revitalize her dampened spirit.

She returned to her comfortable home, called her husband and explained to him that she would have to return the following day. She did not tell him she had seen someone that had sparked a remarkable sentimentality. Collette had a feeling that she had met this person, a very, very long time ago. She had even given him a nickname. And she was tired and ready to go down for the count, 100 − 7 = 93 − 7 =86 − 7 = 79…

Dreams invading her sleep, her God time. Water … water splashing, covering her body, warm with desire. A strong wind was blowing over her, alerting her to the change of life's tempo. She awoke and realized that something or someone was drifting her way. Her Dreamhopper…this mysterious man, this person that had begun to possess her interest. He had joined her, boy howdy had he.

The afternoon was late but there would be plenty of soft California sunshine. She had some downtime and an evening ahead of her—no papers to grade, no lesson plans to be made. She did not feel inclined to speak of her experience, and she had taken an oath to remain quiet. All information she had heard was *not* to be shared with anyone, not even a spouse who was inquisitive and pushy to get the news. Her husband had commented a little about the case, asking her to talk about it. Collette said no. He would not jump on her parade, not this time!

Later that evening, after dinner, Collette realized Elliot had been drinking a few too many cocktails. And of course he was feeling irritable and ready to "pick on her". He was determined to hear the information about the case. His anger and slight jealousy humored her. How dare he become so jealous…of what, a woman doing jury duty? Collette knew what kind of duty he was always away for…"booty duty"

He told her she needed to relax and that everyone told their families about the cases. Collette was tired and did not want to speak of the case, and yet he kept pestering her about it. In fact, after he chugged a few more drinks, he became rude and disrespectful. He was insulting her and informed her her that she would be swayed whichever direction the attorney's wanted. She laughed, thinking she was only an extra...

Finally Collette decided to take the "bull by the horns". She decided to mention that the attorneys were both well dressed and very elegant. She said it to make him a little jealous, and he knew it. He had always kept her close, afraid some other man would take her away. Yet Collette was aware of his infidelities, and he knew that she was aware. He left for the local strip bar... Collette sighed a long sigh and relaxed.

As the night became dark and quiet Collette walked outside to her small backyard. The cool breezes reminded of her of the determined attorneys representing their sides of the case. They were ready to spar. These American warriors of justice were highly educated and used their minds with tenacity and wit. Collette was aware of the seriousness of this courtroom mind brawl. Her interest was piqued by their subtle grandeur and eloquence.

Here were two American gentlemen with the spark of a Southern California Attorney, a breed of its own. Collette felt a twinge of guilt for reacting with the sensation of female longing, not so much sexual in nature but more of a sensual realization. The essence and fanfare left her feeling exhilarated and anticipating the upcoming days—the continuation of the jury selection.

Collette recognized the attorneys' determination, for she was born of the blood of a pioneer. Collette had come to California as a true pioneer, she had been employed in her home state, Michigan for two years. She then moved on to California. Teaching was her niche, whether in Michigan or California. Her pilgrimage to California had been exhilarating.

She took a chance and had interviewed with several California schools at a job seminar. Teaching positions were difficult to find in Michigan, and she just really wanted to do a little "California Dreaming", hopefully as a Mama with a Papa. And that is what brought her to one of the most rewarding experiences of her life—a classroom, a child, a family.

Rising early the next morning, Collette paid special attention to her clothing, choosing to wear a mixed ensemble. She matched a tan military-styled wool jacket with a pair of stylish black slacks. She liked the combination. Her only regret was the lack of a good leather belt. Even though she was twenty-five pounds slimmer, she had noticed her waistline expansion. She was nearing her forties, and life was rounding her into a curvaceous woman. She threaded the old belt and dismissed her insecurity.

Chapter 7: Day Two
of Jury Selection

The second day of jury selection was long and tedious, just like the previous. Again, all potential jurors were asked to answer a list of ten questions, probing their lives—name, age, occupation, city of residence, marital status, children, spouse's occupation, and family ties to the court. This information somehow assisted the attorneys in their selection. Collette was not sure how pertinent it was but she followed suit and did her best to answer the questions.

After long hours, the courtroom panelists were tired. They had all missed one day of work, and the jury was still not chosen. The dedicated attorneys' cases depended on their choices, so all would have to suffice. *After all*, Collette thought, *if I was accused of a crime and I had hired a lawyer, I would want a jury most suited to hear my case.*

The day seemed to drag on, yet she loved every minute, knowing that he was there and she was here, and they were together, two bodies, in the same room, at the same time. She was seated behind him and was able to see him at all times, especially his side glimpses; his slow, predictable courtroom movements; and his much-awaited chances to stand up. Then he would occasionally turn around and casually look at her.

Collette, who had waited, innocently gave him her most erotic back stretch—arms down, head up, stretching forward and up with agility, gently and sensuously arching her long and slender back. She had not intended to stimulate his masculinity, but was only stretching and making a move to relax and stretch her cramped body.

He feasted his hungry eyes on this most sensual, innocent expression of female release. With all his passion, he absorbed her beauty and sensuousness, recording the memory in his developed mind until later,—this lady of love, this epitome of passion, had become a center of his pleasure beyond all sensations Collette waited patiently and sat almost exactly where she had placed herself the previous day, center left behind her Dream hopper.

As the already selected 10 person jury and potential jurors entered the courtroom, after an afternoon recess, Collette was astounded and honored when the attorneys rose and faced them. Although graceful and elegant, this honor called grand attention to her, a convention to which she was not accustomed. Even though she was self-conscious, she was honored to have such a greeting. Her sensuous spirit reminded her that she was a married woman but still beautiful and coyly shy. She was not quite able to convince her goddess self that she deserved the attention of one so handsome, scholarly, and accomplished. He was the mate of her soul, and she felt unable to give him her most intellectual self, although she could certainly give him the button to her seduction, done both lovingly, yet while guarding her feelings with only casual, quick glances. Only he would see her subtle movements of pure pleasure and seduction. No other would actually know or ever understand. He was her target, and she would send him arrows of seduction in evocative and private means done not as an instrument but as a woman looking for a release of spirit, fatigue, and infatuation.

Collette and her Dreamhopper man shared many glances that ranged from modest to deep thoughts. They lingered closely in the hallway, crossing paths, but never speaking or touching. Their chemistry was powerful and it sparked a flame in Collette's heart. They were as intimate as any lovers, yet separated by more than ten feet and watched over by a judge. Everyone in the courtroom felt the elevation of something so secretive and sensual.

This was a supernatural love, brought to earth after four hundred years of sad and hidden persecution. Absolutely no one would understand the magnitude of such passion. Even the persons in the courtroom loosened their ties and removed their jackets, feeling the heat of four hundred years of love finally finding its way between two hearts, to someday beat as one.

The minds of the twenty-first century had no experience of this magnitude, except in the movies—certainly not in a courtroom, where love had so rarely roamed. Here, in this civilized and orderly courtroom in Southern California was a reincarnation of an ancient love, reunited from its lost spirit four hundred long years ago.

Collette and her Dreamhopper, the handsome criminal defense attorney, was her fascination of another world, and those around could feel the emotions but had no idea where they had come from. Collette was frightened and brought

to another dimension of her life. Mr. Dream hopper—
Matthew—was completely absorbed in his professional
objective and executed an elegant demeanor, while she was
completely enraptured in bliss. He knew his limits and
became a man of miraculous power and seduction, but only
through her eyes. The people of the courtroom were happy
and gleeful, yet true and pure. The joy was enchanting and
moved the minds into a higher level.

The guilty defendants felt left out—all these tax-incurred
dollars meant nothing compared to such love and seduction.
It was a rare and blessed moment that few would recall and
remember.

Not Collette; like a scene from the greatest love story, she
replayed this moment over and over again. Only Spielberg
or some other great director would ever understand this
scene of history and love.

She actually felt hyperconscious as she gazed into the
eyes of one so deep and handsome. He had a style that she
secretly admired. With a quick dismissal of eye contact and
a rush of adrenaline, she seated herself and remembered
that no matter how powerful her attraction was, she had an
objective—to remain neutral and unbiased, to hear testimony
presented; that is, if she were selected. He was aware of her
composure and sincere and sustained objectivity. He was
pleased and subtly intoxicated by her presence. Collette had
enthusiastically picked up this vibe with small and pensive
desires.

As the selection for the jury panel was resumed, the
questioning and response continued for some time; many
individuals were apathetic and others downright nasty. Some
were even pathetic to the point of being humorous. Collette
listened intensely and thought about reading the current

novel of choice, a romance, but after hearing the bailiff tell someone to please put the book away, and that the judge would not allow that kind of distraction in his courtroom, she stopped and put her novel back into her handbag. The patience of Judge Hobbs was amazing, but Collette was shocked when told they were not allowed to read.

After what seemed like hours of listening to individuals with excuses, reluctant to participate as a juror, Collette realized the judge did not give in to them easily. He gently probed and remained unaffected by their sometimes tortured responses. This also was a daily chore of a teacher—listening to students who had not completed their assignment. She tried not to smile and immediately felt a bond with this wise man. He knew people and tolerated their excuses. His presence made her feel honored to be selected and able to see the process of jury selection.

The late morning moved quickly, with questioning and quiet strikes. Collette thought about how each panelist must feel, when shot down in his or her tracks and dismissed from the courtroom.

Collette muttered to herself, "That can be embarrassing, I am sure," but truly these lawyers were polite and tactful. *Wow*, Collette thought, *this is amazing*. She began to dismiss the idea of being selected and thought they were almost through. She could return to her regular life of teaching, mothering, and tolerating a crumbling marriage.

Collette continued to listen diligently and gave her mind to the plight of the attorneys. They were ambitious and determined to make the correct choices. Collette was impressed with their objectivity. *That is how they work*, she thought, *and it is their utmost duty to complete that objective with full steam ahead.* Their craft was a very special combination of education, wit, and sometimes empirical wisdom, mixed with serious calculation, vision, and an old mystic wisdom, perhaps a little investigation...such as spying or investigation.

It was almost eleven in the morning, and Collette again thought of her students, beginning to squirm for lunch dismissal. This was always a stressful time of day, restless minds bothered by hungry stomachs. There were several persons on the panel and several still on the front bench to question. Collette's attention began to wander.

She had memorized each question on the jury questionnaire anyway, and had made a valid plan for her answers. With all this time, she had actually thought of a strategy she could use to expedite and finalize her placement on the jury panel. Her attraction to Mr. Dream hopper was enough incentive to spin a web of delight and mystery.

He had the eyes and the wisdom of an old soul, the one that created the spirit of lust in the name of a four-hundred-year-old love, waiting to reincarnate itself in these two bodies. She was terribly drawn to him and found herself completely enraptured in his presence. She had noticed him noticing her, especially as she stretched and arched her long back, thrusting her full breasts to their peak and reaching her long neck to the extent of its reach. This was an innocent seduction. As an avid athlete, Collette believed her body was a temple. A stretch and a yawn were a natural way to help the body wear away fatigue and mental stress. She found herself searching for his eyes and then immediately looking away. She felt like the perpetual virgin. She was embarrassed at herself for acting so demurely. She had never done this before. Why was she so guarded around him? She began to think that she was not going to get a chance to express her desire to take a jury seat. Then she began to recall an incident on the elevator during a quick restroom break. There had been a brief and friendly encounter.

During a courtroom recess, Collette had not wanted to wait in the long line at the women's restroom, so she'd gone to the third floor and used the ladies room there. Her return ride to the fourth floor was interesting; she was alone except for a handsome, tall, slim, salt and pepper hair, well-suited gentleman, who had a charming smile. He asked if she was on a jury panel. She beamed and confidently stated, "I'm working on it!" The elevator door opened, and he graciously let her go first. He smiled again and gave her a playful wink. She felt relaxed and excited, like she'd received a pep talk and sincere boost of self-esteem. It was also an opportunity to speak up and be heard. The men here were of another breed—educated, polite, witty, and ambitious. And to top it off, they knew how to dress and groom themselves. She had not seen that trait since she left her life in Rome, Italy. She had lived there almost three years, teaching English in a small American school. Her encounter with the stranger was brief, as she had been told not to visit with the lawyers in the elevator, and Collette had not seen this man in the courtroom. She was certain he was not on the case, but she kept her distance anyway.

However, not everyone was as conscientious as Collette.

Earlier in the day, right before the lunch dismissal, she had noticed a strange behavior from one of the jury members. She had waited in line to get on an elevator after the judge had dismissed for a brief recess. The elevator door opened, and standing at the front of a full elevator was the DA, looking into her eyes, inviting her to hop on. She hesitated, recalling the judge's request to not visit with lawyers. As she hesitated, a flock of individuals almost stampeded her to jump on the elevator, next to the DA. Collette just stood an observed the situation, not acting, just thinking and observing.

There was only room for one person on the elevator, so the pushy, thoughtless bastards had to shove and push themselves, first around her, and then onto the tightly crammed elevator. She watched them frantically crowd in, their guilty faces looking at the gawking DA. They tried to stand as closely as possible to him. She looked at him, and he watched her with a deadpan expression. When the doors closed, she smiled in spite of herself. The gallant warrior was testing her. How did she sway? Collette began to question the entire ordeal, "Did everything have to be a game of cat and mouse?"

The next elevator arrived empty and with no regrets, she enjoyed the ride down to the next floor. It was at that moment that she began to feel a bit uneasy—it was just coincidence and nothing to worry about. She remembered the prosecutor's comments, the one who resembled the Russell Crowe gladiator of all women souls. He had commented on arguing with his spouse and that she would not give up until she got her way, which, he commented, "she almost always did." Collette wondered why he would bring up such personal information to a jury panel...He was the father of two children, and Collette felt envious of a wife who occasionally got "her way." Apparently, his marriage was a cooperative effort, unlike her own. In her marriage, she felt as if her husband was the master and she the servant. He ruled her completely and with an iron fist. She was so tired of this type of partnership. She had been patient and tolerant, but she was most definitely at the end of her rope. However, this information was probably intended to reap a few female votes. She was unsure of anything.

Hearing the words from the DA's mouth, she made it her joy to spar with him. Colette's mind kept wandering, but then she heard her name called and slowly rose to her feet. She knew this was her moment, and she moved carefully, with grace and composure. She traveled down the courtroom aisle easily, remembering to move her body like a million-dollar model, laughing at herself she did her best not to stumble or do something completely awkward.

As she approached the front of the courtroom, she felt thrilled but not eager to confront the crew. She moved gracefully and placed her long body on the hard bench. Her nerves were on hold, and she had planned her speech long before it occurred. She had brought along her handbag and the plaid book bag embossed in red with her initials, CSP. She carried many things, because she had thought she could actually get some work done while waiting for this selection. The last time she had been called for a jury, she had spent five hours in a waiting room for the jury selection to begin—almost the entire day, with nothing to do but read old magazines and put puzzles together with missing pieces, so Collette packed a bag full of entertainment.

Little did she know this jury selection would have a completely different protocol.

As her turn approached, she called out the answers with a shaky voice but inflected with great enunciation. She flubbed her words a couple of times and had a difficult time talking about her spouse. He was a turd, and she would have loved to tell everyone, so when they asked her what he did for work, she blubbered something stupid, as to not be a clown and put the asshole down. She made it through most of the questions. When she came to the last two, she answered, "Yes, my husband and I have one child. And no, she is not in law enforcement—she's twelve years old."

Her daughter, Sofia, was a handful and could have used some "law enforcement." She would have fits, and her father would always take the child's side. Any kind of discipline was almost impossible for Collette. Sofia was quite aware of her power and used it consistently with her mother. Collette knew the solution to that problem would have been to have another child, but Elliot, had been completely adamant about not giving her another child.

She did not beg him or even divorce him, but tried to be more loving and acceptable of his decision. She did make a grand effort to encourage the hope of conception through frequent and creative lovemaking. She never strayed and remained faithful to the end.

The judge smiled, realizing the innocent humor of her answer—a twelve-year-old being in law enforcement. Collette kept a serious face but bowed her head to keep her composure. Even the gals in the back of the jury panel already chosen were cracking up and trying to keep a straight face...this was a court of law.

The attorneys silently observed Collette's audience, watching the reactions of the others after the humorous display initiated by the lovely and sensuous Collette. Judge Hobbs was stern, but an innocent bit of humor was okay in a courtroom, if it were appropriate.

The lawyers were aware that Collette had actually humored the judge, and they were slightly taken back, humored nevertheless, but indeed impressed. She had actually melted the ice and had a way to make their jury panel "under her influence" of humor. She could be a very powerful member of this jury panel. People with a sense of humor had a way of influencing the other panel members, or at least creating a less stressful environment.

As Mr. Dream hopper approached to ask questions of the new future panelists—all of whom were seated near Collette, on the hard, wooden bench without a backrest— she realized she was able to look deeply into the eyes of the "man of her dreams" and now not look away. She felt at ease. He somehow had a calming effect upon her, yet she was able to avoid him and then surprise him with a long look into his serious, green eyes.

He was concentrating on the questions and thinking of the reaction to the last of the possible panelists. He had planned his questions carefully. He was an elegant man, lean and fit. His hands were long and finely shaped. His movements were polished and natural, not staged. He was assertive, yet cautious. His blond, spiked hair reminded her of one of her students. She was charmed that he could be so elegant and yet playfully hip. *Yowser!* Collette thought. She was enamored 100 percent but decided to relax, allow the chain of events occur, and just do her duty. She had rehearsed her plan over and over again. Now she was getting ready to execute it.

Mr. Dream hopper realized she was nervous and self-conscious, and he wanted to give her every opportunity to remain calm and let him do the maneuvering. Little did he know how she could command an army, or at least the one in her mind? He was thoughtful and vigilantly asked the distinguished gentlemen next to her the long and detailed questions about his ability to be fair and unbiased. He then surprised Collette with a quick question, "Does that also pertain to you, Ms. Peters?"

She popped up her head and stated a self-controlled and confident yes. It was at that moment that she felt the warmest of affection and desire for a man so powerful and yet so sensitive.

Then he messed it up by looking down at her slightly expanding waistline, as if to tell her to keep her trap under control. *Ahhh, the arrogance of the male mind!* Now, like a hawk in a meadow of fat mice, the DA was circling and planning. He wanted to make sure this lassie could keep her composure.

He had begun to feel that the emotional stirrings of something brewing that could be used against his plan. He was slightly jealous and wanted a little of this tasty tart; plus, he thought he had a possibility to establish her on his side of the fence. Carefully, he asked her, "Tell us of your previous jury experience, Ms. Peters, and why you were dismissed."

Bingo! thought Collette—that was just the question she was looking for. She knew how to cast a fishing pole, and he took the bait like a hungry swordfish. No wonder his wife won all the arguments. She replied meekly, "I was on a criminal case and was dismissed because ... they asked me if I had experience with gangs. I told them I worked with children, so I assume—"

"That will be sufficient, Ms. Peters," he quickly interrupted. The room was silent, a sort of dead calm. Even the chosen jury members sat at attention, trying to comprehend her answer. Collette had managed to offend the defendants who were both established as gang members.

There was a hushed commotion at the lawyer's table and immediately the judge asked for a brief time to counsel with the attorneys, which wasn't so brief. The lawyers exited the courtroom via the judge's quarters. They seemed to dash out of the courtroom. There was a hushed silence in the courtroom. Finally the jury began to rustle about. Collette noticed several gals sitting at the back of the jury panel looking at her strangely, as if she had opened Pandora's Box.

Collette was exuberant; her plan had worked, but she realized that she would have to maintain a very level composure. Her blood was flowing like the river Nile after a heavy rainfall. All persons in the courtroom were uncertain, yet instinctly knew something was up. All were anxious to move around and stretch. Some did, most did not. The tension in the air lingered like smoke from a fire. The break was unexpected and lunchtime was just around the corner. Certainly the demands of a jury panel and even those awaiting the selection process could be tedious and stressful. This was a "brain drain" of a job. Concentration was challenged, and the need to sit still and remain alert was a skill in itself. Everyone was hoping to wrap up this selection and go on. This incident seemed to fuel and new kind of confidence. She knew something was going on, and that was spurred by her rocket fueled plan. There was mystery in the air as thick as the Irish fog on an April morning. There was a stir in the air, and Collette knew something was cooking. She felt elated but anxious.

Much to her dismay, her hypoglycemia was beginning to set in, and she knew she needed sugar or protein. Remembering her plaid bag, she pulled out a can of almonds and munched on several without inhibition. Several eyes glared at her, but she was low and needed the supplement. She then sorted through her bag for something light to read that would take her mind off the strange break. "How about...Victoria's Resources."

The judge and the attorneys were taking more time than usual. She pulled out a favorite catalog and browsed casually through the many pages of images, taking her fevered mind off the show that she had just witnessed.

She needed to move the cogs in her mind in opposite directions, a coping skill she had learned as a young child.

After twenty minutes, the judge and the attorneys returned to the courtroom. Everyone came to attention except Collette; she was still looking at her catalog and was completely absorbed. She took a few minutes to change her thoughts. Slowly, she put the catalog away and let out a sigh. She noticed her Dreamhopper sneaking inquisitive peeks in her direction, and one time their eyes met, and Collette felt the power and deep longing. She held the gaze, long and deep, as time was suspended. They were reunited—two souls from some other place in time.

"He was she, and she was he, and together they were we". This was a spiritual dimension, an area few know. Good marriages were sometimes built on this, if one was lucky enough to find that soul mate. Here, they shared a moment so intimate and so together that the rest of the world seemed to disappear. As her attention was caught, she was astounded at what had happened and how quickly it happened.

Everyone on the bench was dismissed immediately, and Collette was sent to take the fourteenth seat on the jury panel. She had been chosen as an alternate, and the fifteenth person, another alternate, immediately was chosen to join the panel. *Strange*, thought Collette.

They were then sworn in and instructed to return in a week for the trial. The trial was scheduled to last about five days. Her confidence soared, and the spiritual union began to take a life of its own. This time, he caught her eyes as the panel exited the courtroom, but she felt shy and nervous, so unlike her normal self, and as she exited this room with a new direction she knew her Dreamhopper would be on her mind, like the air she breathed.

The days that followed were strange. Collette felt as if she were being followed. She would watch through the rearview mirror, and when she drove slowly, whoever was following drove slowly. The little "follow me" game was freaky, yet amusing. She had not had this much attention in a long time. She did not tell anyone and decided to take her entourage shopping and to a favorite library with grand gardens and paintings—all the things Collette would love to do with her daughter and friends. This was not a problem for her, and the "shadow game" became a unique thrill.

After several days, the shadow became a light. Her husband had filed for divorce, and she learned he'd had a detective stalk her every move! He had accused her of sleeping around. He even had the audacity to accuse her of sleeping with the attorneys on the case. She laughed and cried at his jealousy. She had been working extra-long hours at school and even working at home, grading papers there instead of the classroom, so as to help Sophia with her homework. But, Elliot had ulterior motives. Accuse Collette of something she did not do to cover his guilty ass...

She was angry and confronted him. He became angry and belligerent, staying up late drinking way too many cocktails. Collette ignored him but only after she had suffered and felt a double dose of stress, work, husband and the upcoming jury duty.

Later that week Elliot admitted he wanted a divorce. His girlfriend of the month was pregnant and that she made more money than Collette and had bigger "ta-tas". Collette laughed when he told her this, not only was she delighted, but humored that he could be so shallow and so incredibly ridiculous. "Good by, Good riddance, and hallafuckingluyah!" Collette opened a bottle of sparkling champagne, the one she had hidden to celebrate their upcoming anniversary.

With the spirit of the bubbles and the release of a very horrible marriage, Collette polished off the bottle with joy and reverence. This was going to be hangover she would enjoy!

Chapter 8: The Charmed Handbag

Despite the ordeal that occurred with Collette's husband, she immersed herself in the trial. It proceeded without delay and was an event Collette would never forget. It was to last only five days. Because she was an alternate juror, Collette knew she would not listen to the deliberations, but she had come to some conclusions of her own. She had found the climate of the courtroom alluring, and her interest in courtroom procedures piqued her enthusiasm.

Her divorce was going to be demanding, and her daughter would need her. Although she was infatuated with the handsome lawyer, she realized he was only trying to do his job. Her fascination with him was innocent and was never established.

She did not want to jeopardize his career by bothering him. Her husband's news had upset her, but she was especially concerned about their daughter.

Collette was determined to finish her duty as an alternate juror, but she was confronted with another situation that took precedence. Her child had become sick with the flu. Elliot had abandoned ship, left their home immediately, after announcing his plans for divorce. Collette was relieved and frightened by the idea of how this would affect her child. The house was in foreclosure and she really had no idea of how to bring that to an end.

During the night, after the third day of courtroom testimony, Collette found herself up most of a very long night, with a very sick child. She had not been feeling well either. The flu had invaded her home, and she needed to be at home to care for Sofia. She had tried to reach Elliot that night, but he did not answer her calls; he answered only the calls of a new demanding lover. She had no other choice but to ask to be dismissed.

Early the next morning, Collette telephoned the court clerk to explain her situation at home. She spoke to the judge and was dismissed of her duties as a juror. She was saddened, as she had felt a great longing to be a part of this process. However, with a sick child and the feeling that the bug was beginning to affect her also, she knew she had made the right decision. After her dismissal, she became fascinated with all trials. She read everything she could from newspapers and even called a few law schools.

Again, divorce took her mind from criminal court to family court. After several months of working with the court-appointed judge, the divorce was quickly resolved. Collette would have to sell the family house, but she would keep custody of Sofia.

A month after her divorce, Collette found herself still extremely interested in courtroom procedures. She began to think back on the trial she had witnessed. Her mind churned with the memories of how courtroom antics could affect jury selection and trial procedures. She wondered about the many aspects of courtroom antics, even if clothing and other accessories had any effect on the verdict, or if a juror were to dress in a certain manner, if that would have any effect on courtroom procedure. As impervious and light this sounded she was fascinated by this aspect of courtroom procedure.

She thought about the two powerful lawyers battling in court. Their objective was to win, and their success depended on that. How far would they go to influence that decision? Collette's mind continuously pondered this and told her that the job of a lawyer was to see justice in the courtroom ...but only justice that would bring victory to their plea... Colette was almost certain other factors played into the decision.

She began to think of ploys possibly used to complete a lawyer's objective. The outcome of the verdict was their goal, and she began to believe that some attorneys would do anything to see that take place. A term she had heard was "jury tampering." She had seen a movie in which the jury selection was rigged. She recalled her brief experience as a juror. Her integrity had never been compromised and she had never been influenced in any way. The lawyers, judge, jurors were cordial, professional and completely free of anything she had believed could be "tampering" but Collette believed that jury tampering could occur and had probably transpired many times. She was intrigued. Her thoughts and conclusions came about and inspired her new career as a courtroom investigator.

She had come upon an ad for a private investigator position and had taken to it quickly. She had taken eight months of paralegal training but had to leave the program before she completed it. She was soon moved into the investigation of courtroom antics and later to DNA investigation. The courtroom antics began with her concern about clothing and accessories. Were jurors chosen because of their dress, or their actions, or a combination of both? She imagined a beautiful woman who dressed sharp, was calm, alert, and sexy. Collette wasn't really either of these, she was much too fickle. Then she imagined another woman, this one obese and pasty white, but certainly of means. Whose side would she follow? Or was she along just for the ride? Would her shoes and purse influence the decision of jury selection or the verdict?

Collette began to think of her leather handbag, the one she'd purchased in Las Vegas in an exclusive shop on the strip. The rumor was that many famous divas shopped there. Many handbags were displayed in glass cases under lock and key, but her purchased charmed bag was not. It had been on the 75 percent-off rack, and she grabbed it and a crystal-covered belt, done in cowboy-bling style. She loved the accessories, and they would forever remain an heirloom for her daughter and possibly her daughter's daughter.

Now this distressed green leather handbag was unique. It had a charm on the zipper, a lucky horseshoe, and other beautiful charms with beads and symbols. They were interesting, but Collette was really not a superstitious or highly religious person. She was spiritual and did a great deal of praying; she had even attended church services, on occasion. She loved the fellowship and the music. They had a very good affect upon people, creating happy people full of goodness and passion. But, there were problems in those houses of worship...

The crystal horseshoe was an old Irish symbol that supposedly brought good luck and prosperity to all who honored it. She loved it just because it reminded her of her horses. Collette loved horses and had dreamed that she had at one time been a warrior, like Joan of Arc, or perhaps a Goddess of Love mounted on a white horse with long strands of white mane and tail. But old symbols; would this have an influence on the lawyers selecting their panel? Perhaps it would actually hinder their choice of selecting an individual because of the connotation of superstition. *The Irish have a strong view on symbols and their meanings,* Collette thought, *much like that of our English alphabet.* How about the choice of a man or woman's suit? Would that have any effect on verdict or jury selection—if the suit was tailored and expressed great wealth, or if it had shoulder pads with a flair for the military style? How would that influence the court and its decision? *What an idea!* Collette began to consider this as an inquiry and at once began to explore the foundation. She was so fascinated that her studies took her immediately into courtroom theory and writing. Jury ethnicities was also very deep subject... She was amazed to learn of the antics used in courtrooms—the obsession for power and all for the glory of success. What about justice? Did Lady Justice ever call out and order the court to work or her behalf?

Collette's thoughts brought her back to a missing ingredient, and that was of her lost love for her ex-husband. How could she have been so easily betrayed? She thought about how easily love could be ignited or better yet reunited. Love was a powerful force and perhaps the most powerful of all forces. It was not something to play with, or to use as a weapon. The Italians believed that definition of love was extensive and went in many directions. Could love then be a force that never left the earth but waited to be consumed by those truly worthy? How about goddess love?

We speak of God's love in a contemporary religious fashion, Collette thought, but whatever happened to the love of the goddess? Why was that thrown under the rug? Could that be because we live in a male dominated world and because of not wanting to be challenged by the Sacred Feminine.

In the history of Christianity, what caused the great Constantine to begin a new outlook for his followers? Jesus and God were the determining rulers, but the goddess was lost and considered an old myth. Was that done to influence the domination of male over female? Colette's mind raced with these thoughts, all influenced by her courtroom experience. She believed that the female power had been underestimated for so many years.

A man or a childless woman could never realize the power of birth. Even the male who assists at birth can never understand the miracle of power a woman and her birthed young share—a power long dismissed by many but mostly by the male sex, who has dominated this planet for some time. Colette's theory was that the female's power had been significantly underestimated for so many years because of the male's oppressive need for power. Perhaps this was his greatest mistake—to repress this sacred power, especially at the risk of all kind on earth.

Thinking back, Collette's mind zeroed in on the fact that a red-patterned Native American-inspired design had occurred both on the small paper lunch bag she carried and her Dream hopper's tie. Was this a coincidence or plan? Could two complete strangers share a knowledge that was formed from the same zygote, or had love entertained their minds to share this common knowledge? Was the coincidence just a random shot in the dark, or was it, by chance, engrained in science and could actually have factors that could prove its occurrence?

Collette thought about the protocol of courtroom order. Her memories took her back to her jury experience months ago, when she and her Dreamhopper had shared a most unique and thrilling moment in time. Collette remember listening to the droning of lawyers, who seemed to be stalling, tactics possibly used to sway the verdict. These tactics caused the mind to wander. Why was this stall used? Was it to confuse jurors, or was it a ploy to change the verdict, or was it a way to increase time for billing purposes? Lawyers are very well paid, especially for court time. All possibilities marched through Colette's inquisitive mind.

Again, thinking back, Collette remembered she had been anxious, and her mind was moving at a pace most race drivers never experience. Once she had left the jury box, after a dismissal for a break, she absentmindedly left her handbag in the courtroom but grabbed the Native American-patterned lunch bag, her snack sack! She was the first one to exit the courtroom and all eyes followed her.

The bright red bag caught everyone's attention, especially the fact that it matched the tie of Mr. Dream hopper. Collette realized this and was on the verge of a nervous breakdown. Some of the others that had noticed were taken aback by its randomness, but as always, it was either shoved under the rug or taken as a suspicious threat. Not one considered the idea that it might be a display of miracle or female/male power through their shared state of consciousness. Yes, miracles existed, but the idea of one being so simple and so obvious was not comprehensible to the traditional human mind.

After they had reassembled, the courtroom was filled with dead silence. Did they not realize the power of the significance, or were their minds too clouded by doubt that they ignored it, repressed it, or simply concluded that it was a setup to throw off the trial? Ah, *the nature of man!* Collette inhaled a breath of amusement. Women were most likely to comprehend the miracle, but most men were unable to even fathom the theory. But not Mr. Dream hopper—he was very aware and completely smitten by the occurrence, but he had to remain aloof and objective for the sake of his client.

Collette's theories began to grow; she believed in love and the power it created. With clear memories she thought of the the courtroom full of mystery and, to the snorts from the sleeping juror. The absurdness that someone would fall asleep astounded her.

During any recess Collette tried to collect herself in the restroom, but this time only to discover she had started her period—no wonder she was feeling crazy. She suffered from a severe case of premenstrual syndrome. As always, a woman's monthly suffering was dismissed as a form of phobia or mental illness. She had been medicated carefully by her caring doctor but extreme occurrences of stress magnified its severity. In the courtroom hallway, Collette quickly ingested her almonds and hoped they would relieve the anxiety and the strain of coping with her dilemma. She had also become quite reclusive and unable to speak to anyone, yet they all watched her like a hawk. She was a mystery they had never seen before. Some of the men were actually more sympathetic than the females in the room. These men were true warriors of the female goddess and recognized the power within her.

Much to Collette's amazement, the judge had decided to dismiss early that day. He too had seen these signs, some opinions opposing and some contrasting. Universal truth was an old wisdom that had been held in utmost esteem, but had been either ignored or oppressed, as it was difficult to understand and even more difficult to prove. Collette began to suppress the urge to run away and stay away forever. This situation was frightening her, and she was already confronted with the fires of the home front. Her only duty in life, given to her by the commander in chief, was to care for and nurture her offspring. Her child was getting sick and so was she; thus, this was another theory of the shared stream of consciousness that prevailed between mothers and their children.

On her drive home, she remembered the scene outside the courtroom double doors. This was where the four plaintiffs assembled, seated next to the DA. She had watched them through her well-conditioned peripheral vision, another skill she'd acquired as a teacher. She had seen them and was uncertain as to why they were hugging and smooching—it was as if they had won the lottery. This observation was also followed by a conversation that made her question the validity of their joy. Collette sensed a strange event transpiring. This cluster of people was strange and calculating. She concluded this observation was an indication of an unsettled world, where integrity was a thing of the past and people had begun to think of their own needs and desires before the needs of others. Collette, at that moment in time, realized that she had made a strange and profound connection to the court system. She did not know how or why, but the feeling was powerful and began to inspire her to make a career change.

Chapter 9: Collette's Notation on DNA

*A*fter Colette's divorce, and her other experiences with the law, she became fascinated with the courtroom. She was certain she did not want to be an attorney, but she was interested in forensic investigation. After the jury experience and the occurrence of the theft in her apartment, she was driven to "jump on board"

The "petty theft" of her grandmother's ring was the catalyst of her yearnings. Strangely enough, it had started in her apartment, and Sophia was the "right-hand man".

Kelly Armstrong was the audacious, blond neighbor, living below Collette and Sophia. She had also experienced tragic divorce. And so, they struck a common bond and became friends, or what Collette thought was a friend.

Colette's divorce had indeed been difficult, but Kelly's had been a nightmare. Many times Kelly would stop by Collette's apartment with a bottle of Pinot Grigio or a premixed bottle of margarita's (Kelly's favorite). Kelly used to humor Collette with remarks like, "Why mix the stuff, when you can buy it ready to inhale."

The girls would most certainly enjoy their drinks, Kelly would jabber on and on about her ex-husband cop, who had been quite a character.

He had kept loaded guns around the house, even with their children toddling around. Kelly was always concerned, especially when she came home one day and found his guns unloaded in the thighs of a younger brunette.

So, Collette listened, unconditionally to the long stories of Kelly's grief.

One Saturday morning, Collette and Sophia were looking at old jewelry and realized that Sophia's grandmother's engagement ring was missing. They had searched the jewelry boxes, and the drawers, and the entire apartment, and still they could not find the precious ring. They tried to dismiss the loss as a misplacement, "Surely, it will show up, one of these days." Collette stated to Sophia. And then to their utter amazement, they noticed other pieces of inexpensive jewelry missing from its place. The missing jewelry then became a real problem, and then the worst of all things Collette's old Social Security Card, the original that she had kept over the years, because she loved looking at her signature, thinking how wonderful it was to be able to still have this important document.

It had too, been missing, along with the engagement ring and several other necklaces and bracelets. All had been gifts from her elementary students. They were not valuable, but carried sentimental value. Collette was leary and suspicious of Kelly, who sometimes would wander through the apartment... supposedly falling asleep on Collette's bed while Collette would cook up a dinner to sober up her very drunken and sad friend.

Thus, began Collette's schooling at the University of The Rising Phoenix, a school of forensic investigation and paralegal training.

Collette and Sophia had become determined to catch their thief and had purchased spy equipment, such as secret cameras and recorders. And to their much concerned and disappointed discovery, they had proven Ms. Kelly to be a very

Scandalous Kleptomaniac. Kelly had even taken posters, books, and other items that Collette had planned to use in her classroom, before her retirement.

Kelly's capture saddened both Collette and Sophia. They did not press charges, but told Kelly to move out and begin some kind of therapy program. Kelly complied, but they found out later that she had actually returned to her ex-husband, the two timing cop. Well, at least they could deal with their dilemmas together.

Collette's schooling was intriguing and fascinating...she was especially interested helping others that could not speak for themselves..."The Dead"...many times the silent victim.

So, alas she became an advocate, and continued to concentrate on helping these victims. Many times her first lead was the discovery of DNA either theirs, or the DNA of others. DNA investigation became her forte and as she completed her certification as an expert in the field. She found herself contracted by many attorneys, courts, and investigators. Collette also embraced her ability and desire to instruct others about her knowledge. She began to publish small pamphlets and articles about DNA and its use in the courtroom. Her publishing was simple. Something for the laymen, or the ordinary person, just wanting to understand the complexity of such a fascinating science.

***

DNA—deoxyribonucleic acid is the genetic substance that transmits information about an organism and is passed from parent to offspring.

Nucleic acids are long, organic molecules constituted of carbon, oxygen, hydrogen, nitrogen, and phosphorus. Nucleic acids have the instructions to execute all functions of life. Most of DNA in blood is originated in the chromatic area, in the nucleus.

DNA in the nucleus—the cell's nucleus holds most of the cells.

DNA in its chromatin

DNA is a genetic substance located in the chromosomes of the cell.

DNA is the chemical in cells that controls an organisms inherited characteristics.

DNA is the material that determines cell form and utility.

DNA as used in technology and our society

DNA can be removed from saliva, blood, bones, teeth, or other tissues of cells.

DNA testing is time-consuming and costly.

DNA is delicate, and the films created can be difficult to read, especially if samples are old.

Electric currents run through the DNA and sort the fragments by size.

How is DNA studied and categorized?

How is DNA kept and computerized?

Step 1: The sample is extracted from the body or tissue; an enzyme cuts the DNA strand into several smaller pieces

Step 2: Spliced DNA are loaded in a gel that uses electric current to separate the fragments. The larger fragments move slower than the smaller parts

Step 3: After fragment separation, the gel is stained. It is also photographed. When the photograph is developed, a banded pattern emerges that is like a product bar code. These patterns can be compared to other samples to determine a match. This banded pattern is called a DNA fingerprint.

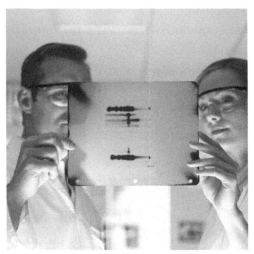

DNA in Society

Today soldiers and sailors give blood and saliva samples so their DNA can be protected.

DNA can tie an individual to the scene of a crime, or it can preclude the wrong person from going to jail.

DNA can also be used to identify the remains of skeletons.

If two species have comparable DNA and proteins, they possibly evolved from the *same ancestor*.

DNA is made up of four nitrogen bases. These bases form the rungs of the DNA "ladder": adenine, thymine, cytosine, and guanine.

A gene is a segment of a DNA molecule that holds information for one protein. A gene on one chromosome can have numerous; a hundred to a million or more bases. Each gene is found at a precise place on a chromosome.

Genome—is all the DNA in one cell of an organism. Scientists now know the DNA sequence of nearly every human being!

Interphase—is the period afore cell division. During this time, the cell develops, makes a copy of its DNA, and get ready to divide into two cells.

Growing—a cell grows to full size; and yields the structures it needs.

Next part of interphase—the cell makes a meticulous copy of DNA in nucleus cell replication.

Important—since each daughter cell must have a whole set of DNA to survive, at the end of replication, the cell contains two identical sets of DNA. At their end of interphase, the cell is ready to divide.

Some species are closely linked—scientists infer that the species inherited many genes from the same ancestor.

Genes are made of DNA; one may compare the arrangement of nitrogen bases—it can then be resolute how closely linked the two species are. The more alike the DNA arrangements, the closer the species are.

Chapter 10: Colette, the DNA Investigator

Collette's research and investigation proved to be a valuable tool in the courtroom. She continued to work as an investigator and discovered some very unusual and fascinating information.

In one very confidential case, Collette had to collect DNA from a suspect for an anonymous client. She had to follow the suspect for a time to find something left behind that would prove her identity. That something was the evidence of our unique self that no one can steal or change—DNA, unless someone tampers with the test results.

Collette was not afraid to be creative and go beyond the usual boundaries to locate and seize the DNA of an individual. As she watched this woman; she realized that the capture of a DNA sample would be easily obtained. She had spied and watched the suspect in the hallway of the courtroom, which was in session.

Collette had been informed that the suspect would be there. So she waited and watched. She found her quickly and had followed her every move. With quiet jubilation, she followed her into the restroom. She was astounded and thrilled when she realized the suspect was purchasing a feminine hygiene product from the dispenser.

With little hesitation and a quick decision, Collette went into the same stall that the suspect had just left. She found a cardboard tampon applicator used by the suspect that had been dropped into the dispenser next to the latrine. This type of evidence did not bother Collette because it was so easily completed. However, it was somewhat awkward and to some, disgusting and foul. This did not matter to Collette. She was meticulously careful, professional, and determined. She was on a high-profile investigation and was unwavering to collect the evidence rapidly and then run the DNA analysis. She did not know the details of the crime, and she really did not concern herself. She had a job to do and was well paid for her work.

She was objective and continued her flawless investigation. The case had something to do with identity-theft concealment. It was an extremely complex and unique case. Collette proceeded carefully with her investigation. With a pair of long-handled forensic tweezers, Collette was able to gently lift the cardboard evidence into a sample bag, which she labeled Specimen 1-A. She quickly sealed the bag and listened to the sounds of the person at the sink, washing her hands. She went ahead and flushed the toilet, so she would not arouse suspicion. She had been in the bathroom stall only a couple of minutes. She peeked through the space between the door and the wall of the stall. She watched her suspect casually primping—applying lipstick, brushing her long, dark hair. It was thick, and Collette was amazed that a woman of the twenty-first century could still have hair so abundant. Collette realized this woman probably had hair extensions and the hair was not original, like everything else on this woman.

Collette did not want to confront this woman but spending too much time in the stall could also create suspicion. She had actually thought about taking a seat and sounding out some bowel sounds, as if she were trying to do her duty. Collette laughed at herself for thinking so lewdly, but she would do almost anything to complete her work both diligently and discreetly.

So few women actually took care of that business in a public restroom. Collette laughed at herself, realizing she did not fall in that category. Collette thought that a bowel sound would actually draw attention to herself. That was something she did not want.

Collette watched the woman brushing her hair, not gently but roughly, and thought, *how can someone be so careless with such an expensive head of hair?* With compassion, Collette realized, *Desperate families could live a month on the money she spent on that mane on her scalp. Oh well,* thought Collette, *I don't need the hair strands anyway.*

Finally, the suspect quickly gathered her things and exited the restroom. *At last!* Thought Collette. There was no other person in the bathroom, and she wanted to lift the fingerprints off the faucet.

She quickly pulled out a gizmo she had designed and patented—a device she could insert into the doorway to prevent anyone from entering and observing her in action. The lift could be done in thirty seconds—all done privately, without anyone interrupting. She took a deep breath, said a prayer, and began the calculated maneuver. Collette was a spiritual person and couldn't have done this type of work without the assistance of a higher power. She trusted God but was suspicious of people who used God or even relied on crime to be their God, so for those reasons she became the investigator determined to make a difference in an upside-down world.

Finally, her work was complete...at least here, in the pursuit of DNA.

***

Collette returned to her apartment and quickly went to her lab. She enjoyed the quiet time in her laboratory; she could work there for endless hours. The analysis of the sample was a tiring procedure, but Collette was thrilled to discover the way the patterns and codes would reveal themselves. She had started the process on the suspect she'd dubbed "Ms. Catwoman."

She had to wait a few hours for several other test results before she could complete the stain procedure. She was terribly drowsy and wanted to rest. She thought of Ms. Catwoman—could she ever use a catnap!

Collette's small apartment was also a part of her lab. Her bedroom was in the back of the building, quietly located and always cool and private. She was comfortable and safe here; a place where she could relax and forget the world.

She had installed a top-notch security system and the lab was only accessible through her loft apartment. It contained some very expensive equipment, all supplied by grants and gifts from sponsors for her much-requested research. She was protective and most definitely wanted her equipment and evidence to be secure. The room was both temperature and light sensitive. Humidity was kept at a certain level, and video cameras were installed throughout the lab (she did this for her own protection and memory).

Each procedure was intricate and followed many precise steps. They were also time-sensitive. She would sometimes play the recording backwards to watch her work being done, making sure she had not missed a step or repeated one. The system she had devised was simple but made her work famous for its precision and validity. It could also be documented and used as proof for any type of procedure that was possibly used for forensic and DNA research writing.

She walked into her bedroom, where it was comfortable and cool. She enjoyed the ceiling fan that moved the air briskly through the quiet room. Sometimes, she would pop in a movie or just read. She was at peace.

She began to think of her career and the success she had achieved. What had drawn her to this point? She thought of the day she had gone to her jury summons and all the events that occurred. She wondered what had happened to the defendants and the handsome lawyers. How about Mr. Dream hopper? She had never been so enamored by any man, yet she did not know him in a conventional manner and had only seen him briefly—those few days in court, once in a newspaper clipping, and then—gloriously—in a news-story production. Collette treasured each of these sightings, and she had saved them in her mind and was enraptured every time she saw them. She was fascinated with the bone structure of his face and his fine hands. And much to her surprise, she had found a picture of her great-grandfather, Papa Cotton, and his wife, Mamal. They were long gone, but Collette remembered them fondly from a picture that her dad had left in an old book. Collette was extremely moved by Mr. Dreamhopper's resemblance to Papa Cotton.

Collette followed his work through his website, and had even painted a "Pointillism" style of painting in his honor. She kept a photo of him in her wallet, to remind her that love can last forever and that chain is truly the only link that will outlive all events.

Her fascination with this man had some scientific evidence, yet she was unable to prove it or even bring herself to him. He was married, she was sure, and her greatest fear was that she would create animosity between him and his wife. So, sadly, she left her memory of him intact, within the deepest part of her mind and carefully tucked into her heart. She wondered what had happened to him. They had exchanged some very sensual gazes—all harmless, a little sugar in the tea. She remembered how he had impressed her with his calculations, and she found herself drawn to him like a magnet to steel. She wondered if he was happy and in love. He was a handsome man with a lucrative career, with a handsome bank account probably located offshore somewhere. He also had more connections than the King of France.

He most definitely was the man of all her dreams. Collette felt odd and excited, but she knew he was out of her league. He was a very educated and mannered man. Collette was a beauty, but she was not willing to take many chances in relationships. Her one marriage had been a failure, and she had tried to date, but the men she dated were never up to par. She found herself comparing every man to this man. She tried to forget him and asked herself many times why she had been so adoring with him. She had never been formally introduced—she had only shaken his hand and touched his arm when she accidentally turned around, and he was behind her. They had introduced themselves only to be sociable. She had been certain that on that day, he had planned to be near to her for a reason. She was very aware of his attraction to her; in fact, she suspected he knew her quite well, somehow. Collette was aware of his profession... investigation, hum... Nothing could ever be proven or would ever be allowed to surface. Collette would take this thought to her grave, hopefully later and not sooner.

There were other occurrences that could never be brought to the surface—like the dream of the man dying in her arms in the strange and dark prison cell. His last words to her...she was saddened and wondered how she had known him, or had she. His resemblance to her own family. Collette realized their acquaintance was but a harmless and powerful phenomenon, and she would live with that, but she would never allow her life to be consumed by this secret passion.

And after all, their encounters had been innocent, and that was the depth of their moments. Collette had to admit that the spiritual exchange that took place in that courtroom would never take place with another man again. She had found a soul mate, an interesting and a once in a lifetime experience.

Collette began to yawn, and warm teardrops rolled down her cool skin. She was more than drowsy, her mind began to drift into a light sleep. The cool air circulated and the room was quiet, with a rustle of wind in the trees and the faraway sound of cars zipping by on the freeway. She was fond of these sounds but her heart mourned for the man... the man of her dreams, her Dream hopper.

Collette continues to think..."This was life in Southern California. She was just a quiet citizen, doing her part to contribute a life of dedication and commitment to make the country a better place for all. Perhaps, she would never be able to love this man of her dreams in a physical way, but conceivably, he would be a part of a bigger experience, part of the dream world, where life was unexplainable and events continued after life as she knew it—eternal life, or life as a spirit, or life with God, or wherever one believes and honors."

Surrendering herself to sleep, Collette found herself dressed in a white gown. She was in a different world, a dark world that was cold and full of black crystals. She could hear no sound, except the deep breathing of her sleep. She looked down, she could see nothing but she knew her feet were bare, and the floor was hard and ice cold. She could the outline of her own hands and also realized she was walking or drifting. All at once, she bumped into a low, rising object. She felt excruciating pain. She had jammed her toe against the object. She, cried out, but strangely she was speaking in French!

This was absurd; she did not know French. She began to feel about her surroundings. She had bumped into a very hard object, and her throbbing toe was a casualty to that.

Curiously she began to explore the dark and frozen world around her with her fingers, reaching out. As she encountered an object, she felt something strange and frightening. To her horror and dismay, she had found a body, reclining like a dead man in a coffin. This body seeming to be as still and silent as any dead body would be. Collette shrieked in silence. Where was she? Who was this? And why was she here? She was alarmed and immeasurably perplexed. She was frightened but curious. Collette knew she was dreaming and became quite alert and coherent. This was a fascinating and wondrous opportunity, and Collette wanted to explore and learn. She had forced herself to remain coherent during these moments, looking around for details that might help her to understand the dream and also to record the discovery like a scientist.

She thought she had touched a body and she was in a new realm of undocumented science. Here she was in her own dream, one that could be recorded and possibly documented and used as a new approach to research in a vast number of fields. Pulling herself together, she began to explore like an examiner. Again, she reached out to touch the body, but accidently bumped her elbow. She could not see it but she moved her fingers carefully over the substance. The wall was made of a gritty substance and was easily scratched, like a sedimentary rock.

Collette's investigative skills took command. She scratched the surface again with her fingernail, she had just taken a specimen and it was embedded in her fingernails. This was a technique she used in tight spots when she was without necessary tools and specimen bags.

Although the surface most likely not organic in composition, her collection technique was similar to her collection of DNA. It was actually done quite easily, but because of its fragility, a structured technique was necessary.

She bent down to the floor to examine its composition. This one was solid and required a harder tool. She always wore a special ring for this purpose, but her ring was not on her finger. She was in a dream. *Who dresses and prepares for travel upon retiring to bed at night?* Collette humored herself. Humor was the one trait that gave all humans a chance to relieve themselves of fear and anxiety.

Collette was now ready to examine the body. Very slowly she moved her fingers over the body locating the midsection. This was a male—chest was flat and shoulders wide. Her vision was clouded, but her hands could tell her many things. She decided to follow his arms and examine the hands and muscles in the arms. This could give her an idea of a range of ages. She had a technique that worked well; it was not specific but nevertheless allowed for a good hypothesis. His arms were long and lean with ample muscle. *He was healthy.* She felt oddly overcome with grief. She did not know him and did not think she knew him, but still she felt the sorrow that one might have upon finding a passed relative, friend, or lover.

She proceeded to examine his fingers. They were long and groomed, not callused or injured. His hands felt as if they were able to work as a laborer but the fineness in the bones indicated he was not a long-time laborer.

With apprehension, Collette reached down to his side, and discovered that his shirt was unique, fitted at the shoulders but billowing in the sleeves. The fabric was course like a gauze or perhaps a linen and it was tattered and was covered with a dried, hard substance...blood!

With deliberate movements, Collette collected three samples under separate fingernails on her right hand and a sample from the wall with a fingernail on her left hand. Collette was determined to continue the examination and actually wondered why she was still in this dream. Her coherency had not awakened her, and she was able to follow the dream and complete a new and strange type of DNA/carbon collection, all ready for laboratory analysis when she had awakened, speculating that the samples would remain within her nails.

The strange and dark world was terribly cold. Collette was becoming quite aware of her discomfort. Despite the fact that she was horribly cold and felt the pain from her stubbed toe, she continued her research. The icy temperatures penetrated her limbs. Her feet were bare and were rapidly losing her precious body heat. She felt the chill of death sweeping through her body.

As she continued her search, she gently touched each leg of the man and made a very odd discovery—warmth was rising from something in his right pant pocket. The heat was strangely fascinating. She kept her thoughts clear and concise, concentrating on the fabric and style of his pants. These smooth trousers were very different, something unlike the fabric of the twenty-first century. The trousers were shorter but full in fit and had many pockets.

She slowly inserted her right hand into the deep pocket. She again felt the comforting warmth coming from a solid surface. It was warm to the touch and immediately brought relief to her cold hands. She studied it and realized it was a ribbon with a cameo. She recognized it distinctly—she had one in her jewelry box, given to her by her grandmother; it was a family heirloom that had been a gift to her great-grandmother after her husband had passed. He had been a sailor. Collette was touched.

This poor frozen man carried a cameo, probably from someone he loved dearly. How odd that it was warm. She moved it around and discovered several strands of hair caught in the clasp. She would take one as another specimen sample that would identify another character in her dream. Carefully, she returned the cameo, but before she did, she brought it to her eyes, she could see the engraving in the pink shell—it was of a mother and two young children. Collette's eyes again filled with tears that dripped delicately upon the cameo. Without a thought, she slipped the warm cameo back into the pocket of this man, so alone, but with the love of his life so unknowingly near to him.

She could not stop crying, and as she moved away from his side, she reached out to touch his face—strong, protruding jawline, high cheekbones, and again, she discovered a crumbly substance: blood. He had, without a doubt, been beaten. The abrasions were also swollen. Had he been severely beaten? With tears in her eyes, she took the last specimen under another fingernail. She was so overcome with sorrow that she felt faint. She thought to herself, "Why am I so grief-ridden?"

Immediately, Collette saw a flashback of the courtroom and her last jury summons. She recalled the warm dark green eyes and the fondness she felt for the unknown man. In an instant, she began to connect the memory with the face of this frozen dead man beside her. She was horrified—he was the same man! She was sure of it. Her tears poured from her eyes and landed upon his handsome face. She knelt and touched him and began to say an old Irish poem she had learned somewhere—she didn't know where, but the words flowed freely, as did her tears. ...

Collette awakened in a flash. She looked around and realized she was in her bedroom.

Automatically, she began to think of her duties. She did not spend a moment to ponder over the

Mysterious dream. She was a professional, and she had research that demanded her immediate attention. Without hesitation, she jolted out of her deep sleep and reached out to grab her cell.

The digital light-up illuminated the time. She rose quickly, not noticing the swollen toe she had injured in her dream. She had time-sensitive work to complete...

She grabbed a lab coat and pulled her long hair into a pony-tail and walked to the lab.

She turned the lights on dim and powered her video cameras. Soft music would be calming, so she pressed the play button of her MP3, mounted it on the speaker system, and began to complete the analysis.

She was rested but felt awkward; the sleep had been deep and sound. With great effort and concentration she worked intensely for the next three hours. All at once, her back began to ache and her foot was throbbing.

Collette decided to take a break. Looking at the dried blood on her toe she went to the bathroom to treat the injury. "What had happened to her foot?" she thought.

She walked to the the kitchen. She wanted a cup of tea. Tea would do the trick—something black, sweet, and topped with milk. As she grabbed tea bags from a handsome tin, she noticed in the bright kitchen light, that her fingernails looked filthy. *What?* Her nails were always spotless ... unless she had done a rugged specimen collection without equipment. She froze in her tracks, remembering the dream. "Oh, my God!" she shrieked.

Until now, her hands had been covered with gloves, so that she had not seen the debris left in the nails. And the dream had been forgotten, but now, incredulously, she stared at her hands and at her nails.

She could not move; even breathing was difficult. Her mind flashed back to the dream. In vivid detail, she recalled that she had been so very cold, dressed only in the long white gown, and her feet had been bare. She remembered the black crystals and ice fog flowing around like the mist that loomed over a lake on an early morning.

And there was the man—the man she had found and examined; this was the man who had died in the cold and frozen dream. She had discovered his body in a dream, yet she had also taken samples to be analyzed—all proof that dreams could be a factual part of scientific research.

Collette felt strangely vulnerable as she moved toward a new and wondrous discovery. Was that where she was? In a freaking, cold-ass dungeon? In all her life and discoveries, she had never experienced or heard of such happenings. Had she gone mad? Collette was both excited and perplexed. She gulped the steeping black tea, forgetting to add the milk and sugar. After several quiet moments, she slowly came to her senses.

Returning to her lab, she brightened the lights but forgot to turn on the cameras. Odd for Collette, but she was so overtaken with the need to investigate this strange occurrence that she forgot her normal protocol. She continued her research. She wanted to begin the DNA analysis immediately.

She scraped the debris from under her nails, placing each on a separate glass slide. Then Unlike the precise and careful investigator she was, Collette accidentally cut her finger on the edge of the sharp glass. A speck of her own blood remained on the glass and would also be discovered later—much later—bringing about the truth and realization that would validate her greatest dreams.

Out of confusion, Collette returned to her comforting kitchen and turned the gas on to begin making another cup of tea. After several quiet, contemplative moments, she heard the whistling teapot as the water boiled, snapping her out of the moment. She placed two teabags in the teapot and poured the water to steep.

She had also decided to whip up some food. Poor a little marinara sauce into a pan, and heat up pasta. A quick and easy carbohydrate...The pasta sauce was boiling, and she lowered it to a simmer.

By now, the water was boiling, so she added salt, gave it a quick stir, and then carefully placed the angel hair pasta into the boiling water. The steam coming off the water in the pot mesmerized her. Had she actually been transported into another world, where she could touch and collect small amounts of debris? If this were true, she would have a case of unexplainable discovery.

Astonished, she sat down and sipped her hot tea, with the addition of sugar and milk. Its warmth gave her comfort as she thought back to the cold dungeon. *Cold dungeon!* The body was in a cold, dark place, a room surrounded by a hard particle. She had the proof of its carbon compounds, if that is what it contained. She would scan the debris carefully and send it to be dated. She recalled that the clothing of the man was of another time—another world.

The pasta had boiled long enough—she liked her pasta *al dente*, not overcooked, a Florentine technique that would forever stay in her mind. She strained the pasta and quickly poured it back into the hot pan. She dropped some olive oil into the pasta and gave it a moment to sit. She sipped her tea with apprehension. Could she have actually traveled in time through her dream? Would this be something she could do again? Grabbing a plate she filled it with hot, pasta, and onto which she poured a heaping spoonful of marinara sauce and then grated the hard Romano cheese on top. She placed the plate on the table and said a prayer—the prayer she had not said for ten years or more. Why had she become so mysterious? She then remembered—her weeping over the frozen body and reciting her great-grandmother's prayer; the man she did not know but who seemed like the love of her life; the man she strangely recognized and loved. Collette began to question her sanity. Was she mad?

After consuming the pasta and finishing her tea, she felt her mind settle and her body relax. She had finally accepted the dream, and the lab analysis would prove or disprove her theory. She would not think of it again. With that, she cleared the table and grabbed a small container of her favorite ice cream. She deserved some type of indulgence, and ice cream would give her mind and body something cold and thrilling.

She powered her television and selected a film from the film noir collection she received monthly. She wanted to watch an old movie, something romantic and something historical. Scrolling through the titles she found a movie, but the title was in Gaelic. *Odd*, she thought. She remembered her best friend, a red-headed, full-blooded Irish Catholic American gal. She would watch this, even if it were in Gaelic.

As the movie began, a young woman was gazing into the Atlantic Ocean from the steep Irish Moher Cliffs. She was looking for something, and as the narration began, Collette learned she was looking for her lost love, apparently lost in a shipwreck or some tragedy. The woman was sad but hopeful. As the movie progressed, Collette began to feel very strange again. In the film, the two lovers were separated because the man had to return to Scotland to see his family and had left the woman in a beautiful castle. She had children—twins—but she was forlorn. As the story progressed, the character began to recall her lost love on a ship; he was a naval captain. The setting of the movie was almost exactly four hundred years ago, taking place during the thirty-year war in Europe. The Reformation was a time when the Catholics and Protestants were at war. Many of them died in prisons, abandoned and lost forever.

Collette felt the anxiety return. The fear and fatigue gave her such trepidation that she was sure she was going to collapse. Here was the same man—the frozen, lost man from her dreams and the handsome man lost at sea in the movie. Collette thought she was insane. She could not finish the movie. She wanted to go out, anywhere to take her mind off this mad day.

The analysis was complete but would have to wait another day.

Chapter 11: Memory of the Dungeon Dream

*A*lthough the dark dream of the mysterious man, dead, frozen in a strange place had frightened Collette, it had also moved her forward. It was the inspiration she needed to continue her research with zeal. She was perplexed by the strange associations she had encountered. All the events seemed to be related and intertwined in a spiritual and scientific connection. This might be the opportunity she needed to validate her beliefs in her theory, which she called the Common Stream of Consciousness, or in her own words, Forensic Time Travel.

She rushed to the lab one more time. She initiated the final step of the DNA analysis. This time, she powered the cameras to ensure she would have documentation. Her result would record her research and may possibly be the answer to the techniques floating through her mind. She was elated yet alarmed, but her desire for the truth pushed her on. The procedure was tedious—she worked throughout the day and most of the night.

Collette was anxious to read the laboratory analysis, but she was clouded by the chain of events that had brought this miraculous scientific discovery.

There was also the haunting movie, the movie near Ireland that portrayed the lovers as they sailed to the emerald green island...

As she removed the slides from the sensitive machine, Collette noticed an extra stain on a glass pane, located next to the one of the bloodied man. She was shocked and fascinated, yet she wondered how the extra stain could have appeared...

She went ahead and looked at the printout of the stain report and was absolutely puzzled—they were of different DNA but each shared similar zygotes. *This cannot be ...* Collette had only collected blood from the dead man within the dark prison walls. Even if that blood had been contaminated by another person, she doubted it would have been female, as this strain had shown to be.

Collette then looked down at her hands and noticed the scab that had formed on the inside of her finger. It was then that she remembered her careless mistake—she had cut her finger on the glass slide before the analysis. It was then that she realized she had made the discovery of the century, and her own DNA was involved in the complexity of the discovery. According to her analysis, she and the frozen man had similar DNA. Were they related? This could not be ... or could it? Her impending thoughts drove her to action...

Without reason, Collette began to think of the cameo she had discovered in the mysterious man's pocket. She was intrigued and realized that another connection was passing through her mind. She overwhelmingly felt the need to locate the cameo that her grandmother had given her.

In an instant, she stopped what she was doing and quickly moved to her bedroom. She found the lovely jewelry box placed in her armoire. She slowly opened the antique box. She had not seen the cameo for ages, but she was certain that it was there. She remembered it was wrapped in a pink transparent bag that was closed with a silk ribbon. She had placed it carefully in the back of the box. As she searched for the cameo, she came upon the bag, but to her disappointment, the bag was empty. Collette was broken hearted. She desperately searched through the box, looking for the cameo. Had she placed it in another bag or perhaps another box? She removed the jewelry and carefully placed each piece, side by side. A strange sorrow came over her. Had she lost the precious charm?

She left the room feeling forlorn and depressed, yet she overcame that fear the moment she returned to her work. In the quiet lab, she ran the next series of tests. She wanted to see the analysis of the crumbled dungeon wall. She could do a rough carbon estimate, which would give her a time period of when the substance was created. As she dimmed the laboratory lights, a sparkle caught her eyes. She looked again and saw the sparkle, even brighter this time. Collette was curious. So much was happening, and she was feeling apprehensive.

She moved toward the sparkling object, and lo and behold, on the table full of electronics and other gizmos was a pink cameo. It was not the one she'd been looking for—it was the one that she remembered from her dream, the one that had warmed her hands, found in the pocket of the frozen man. As she examined the cameo closely, she saw it was elegantly rough but exquisite, unlike the modern-day cameos made in factories or assembly-line jewelers. She realized it had been carved from a pink shell, most likely from the large conch shells washed up on some white beach in the French Riviera. She smiled and felt a bead of perspiration dripping down her temple. Her long, delicate fingers began to tremble. The carving embedded on the cameo was of a woman and two children, one at either side of the woman, identical in size and form. "Twins!" she declared with surprise and a rapidly beating heart. She gazed at the charm, but this time she grabbed a pair of gloves and pulled them on her hands, something she did before every type of analysis.

She then examined the unique piece of jewelry. The charm was on a dark ribbon threaded through a clasp. The cameo was as delicate as it was beautiful. In quiet fascination, Collette remembered the long blonde hair that had been tangled in the delicate clasp. Collette's face lit up. Here was the evidence she was looking for. She located the hair strand next to the slide case, in a specimen box explicitly used for this purpose.

When I run the test, the DNA will easily surface from this hair strand. Then she began to think. *Who will ever believe me? Does that matter? How will I explain the dream and awakening with the evidence under my fingernails?* They would say she was mad and possibly lock her up, but deep inside, she knew, and the Big Guy knew as well, and that was all that counted in her book.

She proceeded to do the analysis on the cameo, the ribbon, and the hair, labeling them carefully so there would be no misunderstanding. Collette had other specimens to analyze, so she decided to complete the other tasks first, keeping a professional attitude. She worked diligently for the next hour. When she finished, she felt calm and ready to sleep. She had lost track of time and had no idea what time it was. She wearily walked to her bedroom, and dropped her fatigued body onto the comforting bed.

As she closed her eyes, warm happy tears began to slowly roll down her olive skin. She was overjoyed, because she knew at that moment that she had made the most important discovery of her life. She had found the man of her dreams and indeed, she had the proof. Would she ever have the will and opportunity to share this information with the world and contribute its spender without sounding like a lunatic? She did not care. Many people questioned the discoveries of many scientists and later rewarded them with honor and contributions...after their death. Even our savior, Jesus Christ. He died on a cross and was persecuted for his innovation and his contribution, regardless of one's religious belief. And Mr. Gandhi, oh my, he almost died for his suffering. How many would suffer? Artists, scientists, children victimized by their superiors. Collette did not care. She was overjoyed because she knew the truth...even if it existed in her mind.

In a quiet and peaceful slumber, Collette drifted away... away on a high cliff, overlooking the stewing waters of the Atlantic Ocean.

Chapter 12: Legendary Love Reunited

Deep in the bowels of the dungeon, Matthew felt the warm tears and the cameo generating a heat in his hip pocket. His heart beat rapidly, as his mind tried to surface from the depths of a deep dream. An angel had visited him, he was certain. He saw her, and she was not a mermaid. She was an angel, dressed in white. She had touched him and had wept over his frozen body. She had said a prayer in his native Irish tongue, in Gaelic; it was the prayer his mother used to say to him. He again felt the warmth of the cameo, and he knew that Althea had visited him. Forever would their love exist. He could not open his eyes, and he could not move, but the light, the tears, and the old prayer warmed him. Matthew uttered with his last strength, "Althea, is that you?" He felt at peace and knew that Althea was near. He wanted with all his broken heart to tell her of his perilous journey and why he had not returned to her.

Standing over him in the white lace nightgown, Collette said, "Do not fear. I am here, next to you, my love. I want to warm you and take you from here, so we can be together."

Matthew reached out and touched Althea. "I wanted to return to you, my love. My death did not stop me. We are again together."

And indeed, his life would continue through the eyes and heart of his kin. Althea replied, "My love, I have never lost heart. I will always be with you, and you with me. As he gasped one last breath of the dark world, he said, "Althea, I ask God to watch over you and your angels."

At that moment, God reached down and answered Matthew with a grand light and a warm room full of people, waiting patiently in a new world.

Chapter 13: Collette's Dream hopper

*T*he courtroom audience was eagerly looking forward, and he had his back to them. He was impeccably dressed in a dark blue pin-striped suit and a handsome red tie with small blue stripes. He wore an elegant white shirt under the jacket and handsome Italian black leather shoes. He was impeccably groomed, with a designer haircut, styled and sharp, slightly edgy, giving him a very hip and powerful image. He was clean shaven, clear eyed, and exhibited nerves of steel. He had the manner of a very old soul, and Collette was mesmerized.

The carefully chosen jury members watched him carefully. Matthew was no longer a prisoner but a lean and powerful attorney, working in the Riverbay Courthouse. He was well known for his work ethic and had established a law firm that was growing rapidly. He had been especially good as an attorney for those accused of crimes that would frighten the devil himself.

Matthew had an objective; he would follow through with" Herculean effort". His clients knew that and so did his opposing counsel. He had also worked as a district prosecutor for many years, winning various awards and publishing many documents that would be available for future cases. Collette was sitting directly behind him. He was not aware of her presence, but he felt compelled to glance over his right shoulder to see who was sitting in the courtroom.

The courtroom was full—perhaps ninety people waiting and listening to the long and necessary testimony so carefully given. He heard an alluring voice speaking from behind him, and that voice reminded him of an angel he had dreamed of the previous night. The judge was still in his chambers and looking to be slightly late, as was sometimes the way of many judges. Their caseloads were tremendous, and their time was critical. Many were already in their chambers hours before the trial, reading and studying the day's scheduled proceedings. These wise men had their work cut out for them. Sadly, the population of judges in the system could not keep up with the cases on the schedule. These were hard times in the country, and crime had a way of penetrating every level of life, be it rich or poor, male or female, black or white.

Collette had noticed the handsome attorney sitting in front of her and realized that he was a man from several years back, when she had been summoned. As he looked over his shoulder, he gazed into her eyes and immediately remembered her—but only from a dream. He was an insomniac who slept on the run. His schedule was always interrupted by a nighttime tragedy. He had to be ready to fly away to a scene, or a jail, or a fabulous casino (his favorite place to unwind).

When he saw her, he was uplifted but slightly taken aback. Where had he seen her? His dream angel could not have manifested itself. He laughed in spite of himself. She had noticed him in a quick exchange of vision. She did not acknowledge his presence, and he was slightly insulted. Many women swooned at his handsome feet, and he loved the attention. *This one is different but odd, in a very alluring way,* he thought.

Collette carried her investigative tools in her leather briefcase and had slipped in a black-and-red polka-dot lunch bag. It was oddly the same exact pattern and color of Mr. Dreamhopper's silk tie. Collette had nicknamed him this because she was both attracted to him and repelled by his arrogance and aloofness despite the fact that he seemed to be in some of her most vivid dreams.

A real Dream hopper! She thought, and he had the audacity to shift his eyes way too often in her direction. She had noticed the tie and remembered the association. Her heart started to pound. *Oh, my God, could this be happening again?* She wanted to run, to hide, and never to be near this man, yet part of her wanted to run down the aisle, take him in her arms, and place a magical kiss upon those inviting lips. *How am I going to give testimony to the judge with "me mind a-flutter" and this strange feeling of déjà vu?* Collette wondered. She had been requested to testify in the case of identity concealment. In a strange and deliberate move, she scooped out the lunch bag and grabbed a hard candy. It was at this moment Collette realized she was in the greatest moment of her life. The candy would distract her, and she could relax and focus on her objective—to give the testimony of a professional, with the evidence she had investigated precisely and confidently.

With her feet, she pushed the paper bag with the identical pattern under the seat ahead of her. She wasn't supposed to have food in the courtroom, but the candy was a necessary evil. She loved sweets and liked to suck on the ones with the sour and fruity flavor that reminded her of childhood. She used to laugh with her best friend about their addiction to candy; in fact, they always managed to speak in a special code, using their favorite candy names. She would also think of her childhood and those long walks home from school, the days of penny candy and the little store on the way to her grandmother's home. She and her brother, Michael, would stop by often and choose twenty pieces of the glorious stuff, taking their time to select the candies. *What joy,* she thought and then remembered their little commands: *"Put it on Gramma's bill."* They loved to say that. Those were the days when a person could actually have an account at the local grocery store. One could shop every day or so and just put it on the bill. At the end of the month, you would settle the bill and pay the balance. *Oh, the beauty of growing up in a small town during a time when people did not have to hurry or stress about cash or even have to drive to town without a cell phone.* Many people had only one land line, and that line could quite possibly be a party line. Imagine that—sharing a line with other families. Collette knew her mind was flying in all directions because she knew, without a doubt, her Big Man had given her the opportunity of a lifetime—four hundred years of lifetimes.

Collette began to focus as the judge entered the courtroom. He was about to call the trial to session. This was a night court, something done weekly to relieve the courts and allow working people an opportunity to go to court without having to take a day off work. Collette pushed the brightly colored bag under the chair again, making sure it wouldn't be noticed, another indication of the she shared with this unique gift with the man of her dreams.

The evening was young, and she did not want to worry. She knew this was one of those coincidences that would be noticed by the suspicious individuals looking for doubt. She did not want to look as if she was associated with the defense, as she was not, but in truth, she knew their connection was of four hundred years. No one in this courtroom would realize the miracle of the discovery.

Collette was elated and felt as carefree as a young girl in love. She felt an overabundance of confidence and let the mystery reveal itself to the people of the court. She wanted to be her neutral, professional self and give the testimony, referring to her investigation of the DNA researched from Ms. Catwoman, as she liked to call her subject. She dismissed the angst and began to listen to the case. She knew her presentation was late on the list, so she wanted to hear anything that might make a connection.

The case was complex, and she did not know anything about it. Her job was to extract the DNA and make the analysis. Her other findings would remain in the back of her mind. She had this priority, and that would always take precedence, but rambling in the back of her mind she could not forget the vivid dream and what had followed—the scientific discovery that could be proven in a laboratory and that would be recorded right here in this house of law. She would have the grandest privilege to begin the enlightenment. Collette, full of emotion, made a secret vow to humor the world as not to frighten them.

The night court session began at six o'clock and ran until nine or ten o'clock, depending on the trial. Trying not to look at her watch, she noticed the overhead clock. It was now 8:45. Somehow, she had lost track of time...

Had she fallen asleep in court? Collette laughed in spite of herself, "I know I am not the first or last." With all the late-night hours and the dark-crystal dream, she had been a little stressed out, and her mind had her working and thinking full time. She released herself of guilt. If she had fallen asleep, so be it. She only hoped that she hadn't snored.

She recalled the gentleman who sat in the back row of the jury panel and that he'd drifted off to sleep and snorted loud enough to be heard by the others in the courtroom. She remembered turning around and giggling like a kid in a classroom. *That was a long time ago*, she thought. She did find it peculiar that the man seated next to her was absent. Had he left? Perhaps he had gone to use the restroom. People were allowed to get up and exit the courtroom at will.

However, she glanced across the room, and seated in another row was the same man. He had actually shown an interest in her, and he was friendly, with a hip kind of style that she liked. He was gentle and pleasant. Why had he deserted her?

Then she thought of the bag that matched the attorney's red tie. Had he seen that? Collette was sure he had and had possibly reported the coincidence. She began to stress, not wanting to put anything to question. This was a court of law, and any kind of unusual behavior or materials were highly questioned. She was actually contemplating an exit of her own, but she had already been contracted and paid to appear by an attorney she did not know. But as she was putting the whole thing together, she realized that even though she had been hired anonymously, she had seen her employer—she had seen him in her dreams, and she had found him dead in a cold prison dungeon. How could she back out now? Her life and research were contained in the next few moments. Again, she dismissed the worry and thought, *Here I am, a professional with evidence that could make this puzzle a little easier to put together.* So without any doubt, she waited patiently and went through her analysis in her mind so that she would be prepared.

When her name was called, she arose gracefully and picked up her black, leather briefcase with the report that would be used to support her investigation. She wouldn't need it, and all counsel and the judge had received their copies. She brought it anyway and extra copies, just in case. She liked this briefcase, and it also contained her much-needed legal papers and of course a small bag of cosmetics, including cherry red lipstick, a hairbrush, and an alluring cologne. All contents were closely monitored as this was a courtroom and security mandated, no sharp objects, no aerosols, no coffee mugs, no marker pens, no...???

She wore a fitted black jacket and a pencil skirt. On her feet a pair of princess-heeled, black Italian-leather shoes. She smiled as she approached the front of the courtroom, thinking of the award-winning poem her daughter had written about her shoes. The poem was done in an animated version. Her beautiful and talented daughter was quite a writer and an avid animation fan. Collette loved the poem and had it framed and mounted to her closet door- "Closet Cares" she titled it. Collette thought to herself, *If I live through the next thirty minutes, I can live through anything!*

As she sat on the chair next to the judge, she looked down at her black shoes. They were not new and hadn't been expensive, but they had been well cared for. Their purchase had been a gift to others. For she was a "Goodinesta"a patron of the Goodwillings. Every purchase contributed to the training and care of others in need, it was also a grand recycling program, and very much a blessing to old mother earth.

Is that not what life is about? she asked herself. *Giving to others, and the true gift will be returned in oneself?*

Collette was ready to reveal the secrets of the DNA evidence but loved to remember the beauty of the human existence, not so much birth or death but the time in between, especially the nighttime—sleep time, the dream world. That was her "God-Time, and each moment was a treasure.

She was ready to express her knowledge to a group of individuals that would determine the fate of others. She was honored to make this moment a sparkling cameo. The one she had found was now delicately threaded on a golden chain and placed around her neck. She would give of herself, and that gift would launch other gifts, thus moving forward through life.

Court protocol began...She was asked her name and profession, her experience, and other questions that would validate her professional wisdom. She was acquainted with this procedure and was prepared to answer all questions.

She gave her evidence and remained ready to receive the opposing counsel. She did not know the case, only the evidence that she had carefully and meticulously analyzed. She also knew of the many dark secrets revealed within her dark crystal dream. These mysteries revealed a world so close and yet so unknown. She did not challenge the truth or slant the truth. The truth was her evidence, and that did not have a verdict.

The verdict could only be determined by the shared stream of consciousness—in essence, the truth that was shared by twelve honored guests, all selected carefully and randomly. When the truth is masked or slanted, so is the verdict. Her honest and precise investigation was the truth. When the opposing counsel took the stand and asked her if she was familiar with the defense attorney she replied, "Possibly." Her voice had taken on a strange and beautiful French accent. The bait was there; why had he asked that? That was irrelevant. Again, he stated, "Are you acquainted with the defense attorney?"

Collette was all too happy to reply. Her courage was there, and she had the evidence to back it up. There was no objection from the opposing counsel, so they must have been curious to hear her response. Finally, she announced her answer. "*Oui*, I am acquainted with the defense attorney." The jury began to squirm. Was this a conflict of interest? And how would that change the verdict. In fact, it could cause the trial to be ceased, and a new trial would have to take its place. Who was this woman using a breathy dialect? Was she French?

The attorney allowed the room to remain silent for some time, feeling the rising tension. He wanted the drama, because it created ambiguity in the jury. He was also feeling the fascination of her French accent. Her evidence had been quite conclusive to that of the defense attorney's case.

She had not known that until now, but this dreadfully dramatic and theatrical display of courtroom drama gave Collette the time to think of the real truth—the truth so few wanted to acknowledge. The judge had a puzzled look on his face, and the jury looked confused and anxious, as if they were ready to jump out of an aircraft at a high altitude without a parachute. Collette was not prepared for this question, but she was an opportunist seeking the truth and the opportunity to confront others for the truth. The strange and fascinating evidence needed to be revealed some way and somehow. Collette would be the instrument. Counsel was armed and ready for the final attack. Collette smoked her invisible peace pipe; she had been told by her dad that she was part Native American, something she could not prove without a birth certificate validating the authenticity of ancestry.

Collette took her time to smoke the joke with a pipe that would remain in this courtroom as a legendary answer. As the "big dog" approached Collette decided to blow invisible smoke rings. If they landed on his nose she was certain he would behave and she would not have a meltdown. "Worked for the kids,"

She had noticed and appreciated his gallantry. He was wearing a very expensive suit and was sporting a pair of cufflinks—and that was the clue ... *link*. She was getting the answer. DNA—the real link to the man of her dreams. He was bringing it to her and the meeting of souls was growing near. As he turned his body away from Collette, she was sure he had a secret message pinned to his back." *Is that not how the game is played?* she wondered. Pin the tail on the donkey?" As he faced the audience and part of the jury, waiting for their expression, he asked, "Are you, Collette Peters, acquainted with defense attorney?"

Collette looked closely at the back of his expensive but wrinkled jacket, trying to examine the mysterious patterns revealed within the creases. She hesitated, cleaning her glasses. They had fogged over from the heat of the moment. The link was DNA. She reached down to her briefcase and began to look for the suede wiping cloth; she had seen this done by another attorney with a good smile and a long lecture. *Ya do what ya gotta do*, thought Collette. She had nicknamed him the Doughboy, in a good-natured way—he was lovable, if you could get to it. A few months of her cooking and they could get down, so she took her time and cleaned her spectacles so they would shine like the DA's cufflinks, less shiny if she reported the strange kiss. Rules in the courthouse were not always listed, but this one was about to list him as a "bar and cuffed playmate."

Collette was flabbergasted when the message began to reveal on the back of the DA's jacket. "Was she imagining something? No, there was an imprint, like a chain link, cuff link, some kind of link!" with the dawning of something new

The DA was speaking boldly to the jury and the listening courtroom audience. This was his show and it was his SHOWTIME. He continued becoming more proud with each carefully orchestrated word. His words regardless of their importance or lack thereof, did not catch Collette's ears.

She was mesmerized with the drawing of something new and exciting. All at once, she realized what kind of link she needed...

When Collette realized that the DA was waiting for an answer she was not aware of, she sat still while her mind scrambled, and yet she had no fear or concern and remained silent.

When Collette did not reply, he began to feel the stress of a change in focus. He had lost his audience. The crowd was focused on something he had no awareness of. The stress filled him with tension, extending down his spine all the way to his groin.

"What the hell?" thought the DA. This bitch was stirring up something." He was completely caught off guard.

Collette saw the frustration in his eyes and realized she had embarrassed this proud man.

Then again, he had been arrogant and somewhat calculating and with that little trick in the hallway. She realized she had just done a female warrior trick, "Rotto le Callione"

At this point, the jury was getting restless and was completely fascinated by the drama.

When the DA turned to face Collette, he approached her closely, and was within two feet of her face.

Female warriors take that move well. A little eye action gets the mind-set. With a louder volume and a forced question that crumbled at the end, he repeated his question. "Do you, Collette Peters, know the name of the defense attorney?"

Without a moment to waste, she replied in a very feminine tone. With a twist and breathy French accent, she took it upon herself to clear the air. "*Oui*, yesth, I dooo. He isth the Mermaid Man, the man of my dreams, my Dream hopper."

Taken aback by her reply with the French accent and the strange answer, he decided to go with it. By now, though, the judge was feeling a little hot under the robe. Collette noticed the look of dismay and complete humor and fascination on her dear, beloved, sitting next to his team of astounded associates. The jury was listening like kids waiting for a dollar. They loved the drama and the twist of strangeness. This kind of theatrics rarely took place in any courtroom. They were all ears. Of course, the defense counsel was trying to keep a straight face, watching the humor in the situation. They knew the cameras were rolling and wanted first dibs on royalties.

As the air cleared, the overheated judge was feeling irritated, a common excuse of his wife after a weekend visit to the local spa hotel and casino. He wanted to clarify the confusion set in motion. He really did not want this kind of drama to go on, but he had to admit, it was entertaining, and he was actually hoping to end his career with a little TV action. He asked Collette in a kind and tolerant voice, "My dear, are you all right?"

Collette was taken aback by his kindness. She replied sweetly, "Yes, Your Honor, I am. Thank you." Then he asked her what she meant by the reply that the defense attorney was the Mermaid Man. Collette replied with honesty and integrity, "Your Honor, I have proof that he is. I have collected his DNA in my body."

By now, Mr. Dream hopper was blown away and had never experienced such theatrics. He was also thinking of the dream with the angel. The dream of a man trapped and incarcerated in a dark world, in which the air had condensed into crystal ice, with no sound except the angel over his body, weeping and praying in Gaelic.

This angel was Collette, and he had not known that until he looked deeply into her dark almond eyes. He was also curious...why was Collette so fascinated at the back of the opposing counsel's suit coat. He, being very perceptive, wondered and examined. The show had everybody

C.S. Nolan

watching this messenger, this innocent DA, just fulfilling is objective.

He had also studied the creases and came to a very strange conclusion—that Ms. Peters was someone he knew from a distant past ... very distant. But he was flabbergasted, how was the connection made? She had stated she had found his DNA in her body. Yes, he was a ladies' man, and man, did this lady have him...

Collette's Dreamhopper began to see something in his own mind. A vision began to emerge, one of a beautiful wooden ship, sailing across the deep blue ocean, with two lovers smiling, watching the sun fade into the deep blue horizon. At that moment, he rose like a gallant knight—a prince that needs no armor, a king without a crown—and walked to Collette. The judge was getting nervous and asked for him to please sit down, to which he gently replied, "Your Honor, take off that robe, and I will take a seat. But right now, I have bigger shoes to fill." With an overwhelming joy, and the confidence of a true gentleman, he approached the quietly poised Collette. He said, "My beauty, you are not telling the truth."

By now, the judge had become entangled in the drama and had pulled off his robe and was trying to fold it. Instead, he tossed it gently to the floor. When he did, the court bailiffs approached him and asked if there was something they could do. He commanded, "Take control of the heat!"

He was suffering from a hot flash! He had just turned the ripe age of sixty something and was going through "Come Chick" syndrome. Some men also suffer from hormone problems, or lack thereof, especially the ones with hefty bank accounts and thinning hairlines.

The bailiffs looked around, and finally found the thermostat, and turned the temperature to a lower setting... They were feeling stoked and ready for action. By now, the other defense attorney and the patient jury panel were trying to hold back their humor and trying not to feel so good. This was a court of law, and the court was watching the glory of the truth.

Gently, the Mermaid Man took Collette's hand and told her, "Your lie is my dream." Collette smiled and beamed her eyes at him. She knew at once that they had finally met. Four hundred years, the love, the truth revealed. He said, "I know you are my Althea, and my ship has finally arrived in your port. Now let's go share some real links."

Althea rose and gracefully left the witness stand. The Mermaid Man held out his arm and gave Althea the escort of a gentleman and together they exited the courtroom. They switched and walked hand in hand and in a walk of unison walked the red carpet exiting the courtroom. The jury exchanged looks of appreciation. They began to clap their hands and the judge sat and smiled with a nod of appreciation... in his pink polo shirt.

The guards were frantically trying to read the back of the district attorney's suit jacket and getting a little too close for his comfort. The DA, both offended and embarrassed, turned around and slapped the guards with his cuffs. They cuffed him in return.

As Althea and Matthew left the courtroom, Althea said in French, "My bag—wait! My bag." Matthew looked puzzled but gave her the right of way. She quickly returned to the chair she had taken, grabbed the paper bag from under the seat, the one that matched the Mermaid's polka-dot silk tie. The courtroom applauded again, and this time with shouts of joy. The hip guy in the audience rose and called out, "They are a proof. Just look at the matching tie and lunch bag!"

The reunited lovers smiled with sincere, tranquil emotions. They laughed and bowed to the courtroom. The cranky lady guard had witnessed the entire scene and was thrilled to see such bliss. Her smile was five feet wide, and her normally gray face was slightly flushed and glowed like a young woman in love. Smoothly and passionately, under the double doors, Collette and Matthew embraced in a long-awaited kiss, four hundred years later in a court of law.

DNA. "Links to the past, unlink the dark cells mast." Ooh-la-la!